Novels

The Lords of Xibalba
The Oil Eater
Blocking Paris
Edge of the Pit
The Catalina Cabal
Exodus from Orion
Quick Read
Legend of the Broken Paddle
Poets and Philosophers

Middle Grade Books

Hunt for the Wild Honu
Hunt for the Wild Taro
Hunt for the Wild Pueo

Poets
and
Philosophers

Bill Thesken

KOLOA PUBLISHING

1.

Los Angeles, city of angels, new year's eve was only a few hours past and the streets were empty, the previous night's revelers sleeping in, while the man in the trench coat walked steadily through the grey drizzle towards the police precinct, up the stairs to the double pane bullet proof glass doors.

His hair was cut short and tight on the sides and top. Not quite military regulation, but short enough that no one could grab onto his hair and jerk him around. They might be able to get a handle on his ears, but he had a solution for that, every day before he left the house he gave them a light coating of lanolin, wool grease, the wax secreted by the sebaceous glands of sheep to waterproof and protect their wool. Every mammal had sebaceous glands in the skin that secreted sebum to lubricate the hair follicles, but sheep had the type preferred by humans. Every beauty shop carried a wide array of the product.

You could get crazy and get wild lanolin from Tibet and pay ten times the going rate, but he just used any generic brand that was on sale at the local drug store. He learned early while wrestling in High School, then later in life battling gangs in the inner city. In sudden desperate hand to hand combat, which could come at any moment in time, the last thing you wanted was someone to get a grip on your ears.

He went through the heavy bullet proof glass doors and stood in front of the eight foot tall framed metal detector.

A clerk with a short sleeve white shirt and a gun on his hip sat at the table with a clip board taking names of everyone entering the building.

An officer in a blue uniform stood on the other side of the metal detector, also with a gun on his hip, and a metal detecting wand in his hand. An additional layer of defense.

The man in the trench coat shook like an animal at the entrance, shedding water droplets off the shoulders of the overcoat, then removed his terminator sunglasses.

The two guards watched him with interest. It was a slow day, no one wanted to venture out in the miserable weather.

"I'm here to see Lieutenant Finke."

"What's your business?" asked the clerk.

"I'm a police officer. I have an appointment."

"Let's see your ID."

"I'm carrying a weapon. A Glock 17."

That got their attention. It was subtle but noticeable. A shift in their posture. A necessary announcement to make sure everyone was on the same page. Nobody liked surprises when there was a firearm involved.

"Is it loaded?" asked the clerk.

"Yes."

"Safety on?" The clerk's eyes narrowed.

"Of course," said the man in the trench coat, his face emotionless, patience wearing thin. He could tell by the clerk's body language that he knew the answer.

It was a trick question. The Glock had a built in safety in the trigger. It was always on unless you were firing it. You had to pull the safety at the same time you pulled the trigger, that way it wouldn't fire accidently if dropped.

The clerk slid a plastic box towards the edge of the table.

"Carefully place it in the container, barrel facing the wall."

The man opened his trench coat, using slow precise motions. The gun was holstered loosely under his left armpit. He lifted it with three fingers on the handle and placed it gently in the basket.

"Is that the only weapon?" asked the clerk.

"There's a few more, but that's the only gun."

The clerk slid another plastic bin to the edge of the table.

"Place all metal objects and weapons in the bin."

The man began to empty the coat pockets. Brass knuckles, a foot and half long billy-club, flexible with a leather wrist wrap and metal knob on the end, good for cracking skulls, a hand held Taser, plastic zip-ties, metal hand cuffs, and two small canisters of mace.

The clerk put the two boxes in a locker behind

him.

"You can have these back when you check out. ID please."

The man in the jacket pulled out a slim wallet and removed his driver's license and police ID card.

The clerk studied them and wrote down the name in the log before looking back up.

"Simon Profit. NYPD?"

"That's me."

"Long way from home aren't you?"

"Thinking about retiring out here. I kind of like the weather."

"You always travel with this much gear?"

"Old habit. But I left the stun grenades and flak jacket in the car. I'm feeling pretty relaxed today, almost like I'm on vacation at the beach."

"Step through the gate please," said the officer waiting on the other side. He was unimpressed by the banter and wanted to get his portion of the job completed.

Simon did as instructed, walked through the metal gate, then waited for directions. The blue suited cop waved the metal detecting wand over and around him, then pointed to a staircase.

"Lieutenant Finke is upstairs, room 201. You can take the stairs of the elevator."

"Thank you gentlemen. See you around."

He headed for the stairway and took the steps two at a time, turned left down a hallway to room 201.

The door was open.

A man that looked to be in his early sixties with dark hair tinged white on the edges was behind the desk, while sitting in two of the four chairs in front of the desk was a Spanish looking guy, slim built, tough and wiry, looked like a flyweight boxer with that sharp glint in his eyes, probably fast with the jab, while in the other chair was a Black guy, thick and burly, the kind you wouldn't want to get too close to, the kind that could put you in a headlock that you wouldn't be able to get out of. They sat in the two chairs on the ends leaving two chairs in between them, which gave Simon a choice to make; no middle ground, if he was going to sit down he'd have to sit closer to one of them. That was the problem when you were late to a meeting.

"I'm lieutenant Finke, this is Fred Pillar, and Poetamos Jackson. You must be Simon Profit?"

"At your service."

"Please, close the door and have a seat."

"Is anyone else coming?"

"Just you three."

Great. He had a decision to make, sit closer to the Spanish guy or the Black guy. He didn't want to show any preference.

Simon closed the door behind him then pulled one of the chairs away, re-positioning the remaining chair so that it was mid-way between the other ones. The two guys on his elbows glared at him. He turned to his right, to the guy with the unusual name.

"Poetamos eh?"

"Call me Poet. My dad was a professor at Stanford, he taught Shakespeare."

Simon scoffed. "That's hard to believe."

"Why," said Poet, his eyes narrowing, his

voice sharp. "That a black man could teach Shakespeare at a major college?"

"No," said Simon. "It's hard to believe he didn't name you after one of the Bard's characters."

"Like who?" said Poet. "Name one."

Testing him.

Simon didn't like being tested. Especially when it came to Shakespeare.

"Like Hamlet, or Romeo," he replied stating the most memorable names. Then with dull eyes. "Or Puck."

Poet nodded with a tiny bit of mirth in the corner of his own eye. "Robin Goodfellow from A Midsummer Night's Dream. The mischievous jester. How'd you know about him?"

"Neighing in likeness of a filly foal; And sometime lurk I in a gossip's bowl," said Simon.

"It's a good line," said Poet. "Lurking in a gossip's bowl. My dad used it often to admonish us kids from talking stink about someone. How'd *you* come across it?"

"I can read," said Simon. "Sometimes I read old books. Because sometimes old lines are better than any of the new ones. Your name however is a new one, how do you spell it?"

"It's two names. An amalgamation if you will. Poet, and Amos with an A. My parents couldn't figure out what to name me when I was born and decided to invent one by combining the two."

"That makes sense. You people seem to like unique names."

Poet clenched both his right fist and his lower jaw while shifting his weight in the chair.

"What do you mean 'you people'? Maybe you should explain yourself before we need to step outside."

"Oh take it easy. I mean you college educated people. Professors inventing names for their children. I thought maybe the second half of your name was Emos, or Imus. But Amos, now that's an old name."

"From the Prophet Amos. From Latin, Greek, and Hebrew, literally 'born from God'."

"I read the Book of Amos last week. He was a forebearer of doom. Amos can also mean a burden you know."

"Don't you worry about me being a burden pal. I can take care of myself."

Finke and Pillar were dumbfounded, looking back and forth between the two verbal combatants. As far as anyone knew, they'd only just met for the first time and yet it seemed as though they were either best friends for years and used to this type of banter, or sudden mortal enemies that wanted to get into the ring, or the middle of the street and duke it out.

Finke patted his hand loudly on the desk for attention.

"Okay, okay, let's get this out of the way right off the bat, I don't want to waste anyone's time. I don't have all day to dance around the subject, and I don't want any half answers. Do any of you guys have any racial preference or prejudice about working with someone that has a different color skin. I have a Black man, a White man, and a Filipino, so let's have it now, any problems?"

Poet looked across Simon towards Fred.

7

"I thought you were Chicano."

"Yeah, I get that a lot."

"He's a twofer," said Finke. "He blends right in with the Chicanos and the Filipinos."

"Filipino gangbangers? There such a thing?" asked Poet.

"You'd be surprised. What about you?" said Finke, looking directly at Simon, who frowned.

"Why ask a general question to everyone, and then specifically to me first? Because I'm the only white guy in this room? I'm automatically a racist because of the color my skin? What if I tell you I'm not a racist because I hate everyone equally."

"Just answer the question."

"Sure," said Simon. "I'll answer the question with an analogy. You know what that is right?"

He looked directly at Poet who shook his head in pity before answering the question.

"You mean the linguistic thought process of transferring meaning from one separate subject to another with the same conclusion? The relationship between the source and the target and the similar nature of the two?"

"Sure," said Simon. "Something like that."

Poet spread his hands out.

"Well, let's hear it. The fateful analogy."

Simon nodded and began.

"I was born in Nashville which is supposed to be a fun city to live in. A lot of country music and good times. When I was seven years old a couple of black teenagers chased me down, threw me in a trash can, dragged it onto the railroad tracks and lit it on fire. Their real beef was with another kid on the block but that kid could run a lot faster, so they grabbed me instead."

"That's a heck of a story," said Poet. "I've got a few of my own if you have a couple of hours to listen. The colors switch sides but the story is pretty much the same."

"The reason I'm telling you this," said Simon. "Is that a whole bunch of years later when I was working as a bouncer at a club downtown, a couple of drug dealers tried to get me out of the way by putting a bullet in my head. I wouldn't let them in the club to do one of their little deals and they were pissed off. So one of them snuck up behind me and had the barrel of a gun pointed at the back of my head, finger on the trigger ready to pull it, and a black woman who was standing nearby pushed me out of the way just in time."

"Two sets of black people acting differently," said Poet. "Just amazing. What about the drug dealers? What ethnicity were they? Don't tell me they were also black"

"Filipino."

They both looked at Fred Pillar and laughed.

"Sure you're both laughing now," said Fred. "Which tells me that neither one of you is from L.A."

It was true. Simon was from New York, and Poet was from San Francisco.

"You telling me there's big problem with Filipino gangs here in Los Angeles?" asked Poet.

"Trouble comes in all colors," said Fred.

Their conversation fizzled to nothing and all three looked silently at Finke.

"Why don't you just get down to brass tacks and tell us why we're here," said Simon.

Finke nodded.

"Yes. Now that everyone's gotten to know each other a little. It's time we got down to business. As you all know, last month I sent a request to the chiefs of the NYPD and SFPD for any of their agents who might want to do a short stint out here in L.A. I needed two unknown entities that could work undercover. Two agents who didn't mind working late and getting a little dirt under their fingernails. Two agents who haven't been seen around here. I didn't care if I came off as racially insensitive or quota minded. I needed one black agent and one white. The world that we live in dictates that we need to have diversity in all aspects of our business dealings. Not because it's fair and right, but if one of you guns down a white suspect, or a black one, we can have a group photo of your team and skate under the public race baiters."

"You said you wanted two agents who haven't been seen," said Simon. "Why did you have us walk in the front door?"

"And you'll go right back out the front door. I want people to wonder who you are."

He waited a moment for that to sink in.

Simon's eyes narrowed.

"You want people to wonder who we are. Okay fine. I'm used to that. What people in particular, the ones on the outside, or the ones on the inside?"

Finke looked at the eyes of each of the men seated in front of him. Simon was the quickest to the punch on figuring it out, but he could tell by each of their expressions that they were all intrigued by the question.

"It's true that today with the sophisticated nature of the criminals we're up against, they use surveillance against us just as much as we use against them. With the kind of money involved, and the penalties for breaking certain laws, especially the ones that bring them the biggest paydays, they'd be stupid not to know who they're up against. Who's trailing them. Who's planting wires on them, watching from windows. They have a database just like we do, the big players anyways, the ones we're after. If there's someone on the outside taking notes on who's coming in to this building, then of course they have pictures of each and every one of you, and are busy researching who you are. This is something we have to acknowledge, realize and plan for, so to answer your question I want people on both sides to wonder who you are."

Poet was next on the line.

"You're acknowledging and planning that someone on the outside might be tracking us. You're also wondering if someone on the inside is doing the same thing. You got a dirty cop in here?"

Simon looked sideways at Poet.

"Is the earth round?"

Poet turned his head slowly to look straight into Simons eyes.

"I don't like your tone of voice."

"All I'm saying is that if we're going to work together, and work well, we have to be honest with each other right off the bat, and any honest cop who's worth his weight in donuts will tell you that of course there's dirty cops. You know it and I know it, and obviously Lieutenant Finke here thinks they have a problem."

"Let me rephrase my question," said Poet. "Do you think that you have an active dirty cop in here? In this specific precinct."

"We're not sure. That's why we got the okay to bring you guys in from the outside."

"You asked for permission," mused Simon.

"I work in a hierarchy, there's a chain of command."

"Most precincts I've worked at were dictatorships," said Simon.

"Only one other person knows that you're here. The chief of police, and his credentials are impeccable."

"Who's idea is this?" asked Simon.

"It came from the top," said Finke. "Should I continue?"

Simon nodded and folded his hands.

"There's two edges to this mission, if you decide to take it. One is for you to break up a little drug importing ring, and the other is for us to find out if someone on the force is involved."

"Sounds like we're fish bait on the end of a hook," said Poet.

"You can get out anytime you want," said Finke. "There's the door. We'll find someone else."

"I'll hear you out," said Poet settling his wide frame back in the chair.

"How little is this drug ring we're talking

about?" asked Simon.

"We're not really sure. It could be a couple of rookies trying to make some extra pocket money and not realizing what they're getting into, or it could be the tip of an iceberg. We got a lead from a reliable source, one person of interest who mentioned a shipment coming into the port of Long Beach on a freighter in two weeks, and that's why we need you guys to step in and see what you can find out."

"Doesn't make sense bringing us in from the outside," said Poet. "We don't know the streets."

"That's why we have GPS," said Simon. "It's impossible to get lost here."

"When I say streets, I don't mean the physical location of the asphalt, I mean the people walking on them."

Finke pointed to the right.

"Fred grew up here. Born in Compton where he lived till he was seven, then his family moved all around this little town. Alhambra, South Pasadena, West Covina, Glendale, Burbank."

"Beautiful downtown Burbank," said Fred. "Seems like I was in a new school every year. It was like I was a military kid. When you're a kid you can get away with a lot of stuff. Fortunate or not, I know just about every back street and alley in Los Angeles."

"He's your tour guide. Graduated from Montebello high school, golden gloves boxer. Almost made it to the pros. He's been working in Denver, in the metro. I brought him in last month in anticipation of forming an undercover squad."

"Hey, I was golden gloves too," said Poet.

"Yeah? When was your last fight?"

"When I was one eighty. About five years and twenty pounds ago. You?"

"Last week. Three rounds. Trying to stay in shape."

"Oh yeah? How'd you do?"

"TKO."

Poet tilted his head in question.

Fred nodded. "The other guy got TKO'd"

Simon kept silent and stared at the edge of the desk in front of him. The ring he trained in had no rules, no referees. A lot of times it was at night when it was hard to see. Best to keep it to himself for now.

"So we're all good?" asked Finke.

"I'm in," said Poet.

"No problem here," said Simon.

"Let's go," said Fred.

"Should we all put our hands together like the three musketeers?" asked Simon.

No one laughed. Poet glared.

"Okay," said Finke. "Let's get after it." He pulled out a folder, opened it and began laying photos on the desk.

"It's pretty simple. You've got three guys. Three knuckleheads. Nick Fangano, Craig Balmores, and Jack McDermott. All friends. Grew up together in Seal Beach. Nick and Craig are thirty eight years old, Jack's thirty nine, but they all graduated from Long Beach High School the same year. Nick and Craig are married with kids, Jack's single, and they all work at the port in Long Beach in different capacities. Jack's dad,

Blackie was the union boss and got them all jobs when they were eighteen years old. They've been working on the docks for the past twenty years, making great money, fully entrenched in the system, not a problem in the world, but they got greedy. And stupid. No one ever would have questioned their integrity and they could have retired in a few years with a ton of money in their bank accounts. But someone overheard them talking. Someone that we pay to listen in on people."

"A squeal," said Simon.

"A trusted informant," countered Finke.

They all leaned forward to look at the photos. Poet shrugged. Beefeaters and beer drinkers with fat cheeks and fake tough guy smiles. They looked soft.

"But these aren't the guys we're really after," said Finke.

He pulled out some more photos and laid them out. These guys didn't look soft. They looked hungry, vicious, demented. The edges of their eyes twisted in wrath, the centers black hardened beads lacking a trace of warmth.

"I'll text you these photos so you have them on file. These five men are newcomers to the scene. Four of them are Peruvian imports from our southern border, and one is from Honduras. Entrepreneurs if you will. We think the Honduran is the ring leader and has the seed money to start this little enterprise. Our three dock workers each got a down payment of twenty grand cash, and they'll each get another hundred when the shipment passes customs inspection. Their job is to make sure that it happens, and to alert these five guys when it does."

"What's in the shipment?" asked Simon.

"We don't know for sure."

"Maybe it's a big bomb," said Poet.

"We pretty sure it's drugs," said Finke. "But here's where it gets complicated. The shipment isn't intended for these five guys. Like I said, they're entrepreneurs, interlopers. They're going to hijack it from the gang that's importing it, and sell it themselves."

Simon sat back in his chair, his interest level increasing. "How do you know?"

"Because they've done it once before and we think they're going to do it again. They figured out a system. Somehow they've got their own intel network set up. They don't have to take the trouble to ship it themselves, they just steal it from the guys that do. About a month ago we had a line on a mule coming through on a cruise liner. An ex-Army Ranger that no one would suspect with some trinkets that he picked up in Panama. Some trinkets filled with ten pounds of heroin, and half a million cash. We had our guys in place ready to nab the people that were picking up the shipment, and before we could move in, these four guys rolled him."

"What do you mean rolled him. Is he still alive?" asked Fred.

"You see the looks on these guys faces?" said Finke. "Of course not. They cut him up and threw him overboard. We've got it on the ship's surveillance tape. It happened when they were being towed to the docks by the tug boat. They tossed the body in the ocean, and the trinkets to a fast boat that was trailing the ship, and then they must have slipped off the boat sometime after that."

"If what you're saying is true," said Simon. "Then we're not the only ones looking for these guys."

"There are some pretty pissed off people who missed out on that shipment. That, and we don't know if someone in our department had anything to do with it. At this point in time we can't trust anyone. That's why I decided to bring you guys in. No one else knows about you."

"I still wish we wouldn't have come in that front door," said Simon.

"The ship is still a week and half out and we've probably got another three days after that before it docks," said Finke. "That gives you about two weeks, should be plenty of time for you to get set up and be ready. There's also a clog in their system from what we've heard. They don't have enough manpower to unload the ships that they have in line, and they've got a few ships anchored offshore waiting for their turn. A lot of pissed off shipping companies that are running behind schedule. That'll make it easier to get you guys on a crew and blend in. I've got dock credentials for you, and you can access the port at will. Poke around, see what you can find out, and report back to me, and only me."

"If two of these guys rolled an Army Ranger, then these three dock workers are in real trouble," said Poet.

"Yeah," nodded Finke. "They've got more than their little jobs and their freedom on the line. So here's how it's going to work. You three will be working on your own, without any oversight from the department except for me. Officially, as far as anyone is concerned, you're on vacation from your regular jobs. You're just here in California to look around, to sightsee, get a suntan. Unofficially you're working for our undercover narcotics division. If you get in trouble, the department will officially disavow any and all knowledge of our arrangement. Unofficially we'll take care of you."

"What do you mean if we get in trouble," said Poet.

"The usual. Someone gets hurt. Someone gets killed," said Finke.

"Things happen when you go sticking your nose in places where you shouldn't," said Simon.

"This is the only way we can work it," said Finke.

"So you think someone in your department might playing both sides of the field?" asked Poet.

"You can never tell. Can you?"

"Why don't you just put out an all-points bulletin, find these guys and bring them in for questioning? Break some knuckles and get them to talk," said Simon.

"How long you been in this business?" asked Finke.

"It's a question that has to be asked," said Simon.

"Sounds like we're getting set-up," said Poet.

"Let's get back to the five guys who rolled the Ranger," said Simon. "You got any other intel on these guys except for a couple of pictures and their country of origin."

"We matched their photos with the CIA's database. Other than that, nothing. We know they're in the country, and that they didn't come in through the front door like they were supposed to. They're here, but we don't know where. It's like they're invisible."

"How do you even know it's these guys who made the offer to the dock workers?" asked Simon.

Finke nodded appreciatively.

"I was hoping one of you would ask that question. One of the dock workers was stupid. He made a large cash deposit at his local credit union."

"And?"

"The general public doesn't realize that large cash deposits are scanned through a machine. Anything over five grand gets the microscope. Homeland security regulations. The numbers on the bills triggered an alert in our system."

Fred had been silent the whole time, listening, taking it all in.

"The Ranger," he said.

"Yes," said Finke nodding. "You see the Ranger was one of our agents. The half million in cash was evidence, it was bait. All the serial numbers scanned and recorded. Once we identified the people picking up the heroin and the cash, all we had to do was wait until they did something with the money, and we could widen our net. Find out who they were paying."

"Kind of like fishing," said Simon.

"Yeah, that's right," said Finke. "You can cast out a single line and catch one fish, or you can wait until they're all balled up, throw the net and catch the whole school."

"Sometimes, even with a net, if you get too greedy and try to catch the whole school, the net gets busted and you have no fish and no net."

"How do you know that the guys who rolled the Ranger didn't give the marked money to someone else?" asked Poet. "And the new guys bribed the dock workers."

"We don't," said Finke. "That's where you come in. You're undercover. No one knows about you down here in L.A. but me."

"And the guys at the front gate who checked me in," said Simon.

"They're clerks," said Finke. "They know you came to see me. They don't know why. When you leave, you disappear. It's a big city, easy to get lost. You're undercover but you'll have access to all of our on-line tools. DMV, arrest logs, mug shots, court documents, property records, land records, tax filings, vital records, marriage licenses, birth certificates."

"Bank account and social security numbers?" asked Simon. "I can get the mother's maiden name from the birth certificate."

"Funny guy," said Finke.

Simon didn't smile. "Not in a clinch."

Finke gruffed. Then continued.

"You'll check in with me only if you need something. If anyone asks, you're here on vacation, and if they get real nosy and find out that you're cops, you can say you're also here to attend the police conference at the Long Beach Convention Center next week. We're having a little training exercise in crowd control. That is a fact."

Finke almost managed a wry smile. He was getting ready to cut them loose into the city. Like a pack of hunting dogs, bloodhounds on the chase, ready to be unleashed, except these dogs all looked different.

"You can call yourself the diversity squad."

Poet shook his head while looking at the ground then lifted his chin and narrowed his eyes at Finke.

"I don't like that word," he said. "Drives me up the damn wall."

The other three men looked at him with interest. They were intrigued.

"Explain," asked Simon.

"It's from Latin. Diversitas. It means various, different, with roots in cultural anthropology. But the meaning's been watered down, misused to control the masses, to subjugate segments of the population. It's used by a wide swath of so-called academics, elites who consider it their duty to regulate humanity to their liking. I can envision some precious society prima donna at an Ivy League college drinking tea with their little pinky finger in the air preaching it to a class full of lemmings. The college where my Dad teaches has a brochure with a cute little picture on the front page that implies that diversity is a bunch of kids with different colored skin sitting around on a lawn. That's pandering in my opinion. And his too by the way. If you want to talk about actual human genetics, there's more diversity between individuals than between populations. I don't buy into the race card unless you're talking about the entire human race. There's no such thing as sub-races. If you try to reclassify people into the white race or the black race then you're trying to say we, or you, are a subspecies. It's a convenient way to put people into little boxes, a handy way to categorize people so you can suppress them. Diversity is code for a cattle prod and a cage."

"I'm with you there," said Simon. "When I look at you I don't see a black man, and when I look at Fred over here I don't see a brown man, I just see a man. But I'll tell you something else right now and this is the truth, when I was growing up, just about every year we'd get a house at the beach for a couple of weeks and I'd get so damned sunburned the first couple of days that I wished I was black."

Poet chuckled and shook his head.

"Damn poor white boy."

"But you and I and Fred know," continued Simon. "That even though we may or may not be racist, there's a whole lot of people out there who most definitely are. We're getting thrown together into a little melting pot and we're going to have to watch each other's backs out there."

Finke stacked all the pictures and pages, put them back into the folder and pushed it across the desk.

"You have three guys to monitor. My advice

would be to go together for the initial reconnaissance, and then each of you take one subject and follow them. But you do whatever you want. As far as I'm concerned you're on your own."

They were all silent for a moment, then Finke ended the meeting with a wave of his hand.

"And now you disappear."

2.

Two men came into Finke's office after his three new hires left. A tall man with thinning black hair who combed it sideways to hide the bald spot on top, lieutenant Chubb, and a thick heavy set man with short stubby blond grey hair, lieutenant Boggs. Both of them wore white dress shirts with black ties, standard office wear in the division.

Finke took a sip of coffee and shuffled through the papers on his desk, setting them to the side in sections. Then he looked up at the two men who were settling in to their chairs, getting ready for their daily face to face meeting.

"Anything on the Culverson case?" he asked neither one in particular.

"Nate Culverson made bail yesterday," said the burly guy, taking the lead. "His girlfriend picked him up and took him back to their apartment in La Mirada. While she was inside the prison signing papers we used our warrant and put a wire in the car, and also in the apartment. Now we wait."

"Who were the three guys who just left?"

asked the thin man named Chubb.

"Friends of mine. They're here on vacation," lied Finke.

He watched them both for a reaction. Which one of you is it, he wondered. Which one of you bastards is going for the golden ring? Maybe it wasn't one of them after all, maybe it was one of their agents who was digging around, sticking their noses in places that they shouldn't be. Someone was digging around. He could feel it. The Ranger getting axed wasn't the only drug bust gone bad in the past few years. It happened all the time. It was the way it happened that gnawed on Finke's mind. The simple fact that it wasn't supposed to happen at all.

"Let's get back to Mr. Culverson," said the thin man, changing the subject, putting them back on track. "Anyone who can post half a million dollar bail is someone to be taken serious.

"You think he's a flight risk?"

"I think he's got a big target on his back."

"Who do we have on surveillance?"

"Connor and Brik are rotating. Eight hour shifts."

"What else we got? Anything new?"

"Clyde Oshimi's coming in from Japan tomorrow to see the heavyweight fight in Vegas. He's got two nights at a Beverly Hills hotel before heading to sin city. He's bringing his new girlfriend."

"What do we have on her?" asked Finke.

"Nothing yet. All we know is she's an Asian bombshell who likes to dye her hair blond, and her father was a well-known Yakuza back a few decades."

"What do you think the chances are she's still connected."

"A hundred percent."

"Pretty sure of yourself."

"She's with Clyde Oshimi. Biggest drug kingpin this side of Osaka. Doesn't get any more connected than that."

"Any news on the Ranger who got whacked on the cruise liner?" asked Chubb.

"The feds took over the case," said Finke. "We've already gone over this. The cruise liner was flying a Dutch flag. It's out of our jurisdiction. We're out of the loop. I can't get any info on it."

"It happened in the port of Los Angeles," said the thin man. "Should be our case."

"International flagged ship under way. Feds have authority."

"A hundred yards from the dock, being towed by a city of Los Angeles licensed tug boat. We should have pressured them on that Doug."

"You have control issues."

"Damn right I do. I don't like unanswered questions. It's why I'm a cop."

"I don't like it either but we have to move on. You've been a cop long enough to know we can't solve every case in the world."

"Yeah, well I was connected to that case. My team worked on it for close to a year. Not only that it's the third sting I lost in the past couple of months. My odds are going down."

"Get a line on Oshimi, that'll make you feel

better."

"I'm working on it." He looked at his watch. "In fact I'd better get going. We have a team meeting in about an hour in the city."

He got up and walked out the door closing it behind him.

"What do you think?" asked Finke.

"About Chubb? He'll be alright. Give him some time, right? He's just re-directing his anger in my opinion. He'll get back on track."

"Wives aren't cut out for this business. I don't blame a single one of them for getting out while they can."

The thick man studied Finke for a moment, not sure what to say. After all, Finke's wife also left him a few months ago.

"All I know," said Boggs. "Is that I feel sorry for anyone connected to Clyde Oshimi if they come up against Chubb in the frame of mind he's in."

3.

Simon retrieved his weapons from the guard at the front entrance. Fred and Poet had gotten theirs before him and were already walking down the steps.

The two men were walking far apart from each other as though they were strangers heading their own way. Walking in different directions. The faint drizzling rain had stopped and the morning sun was trying to break through the clouds to the east. Rays of light beaming sideways towards the earth.

Somewhere far away, the sound of a church bell clanged eerily, beckoning the faithful to gather around. Simon looked at his watch. It was eight o'clock. They'd been in their meeting for over an hour.

After they left Finke's office the three of them huddled up in the hallway, and made plans to meet up at a big box building supply store a few blocks away.

"It's next to the mall and is a busy place," said Fred. "But it has a lot of parking. No one will notice or care if we leave our cars there all day. Let's meet there at the southwest corner, and take one car to the docks."

And then they split up to leave the building.

If Finke was right and someone on the outside was monitoring who came and went from this building there was no sense giving them anything the easy way.

Three men leaving the building at approximately the same time and walking in different directions at eight o'clock on a Sunday morning should be no cause for conspiracy theories.

Still, Simon paused at the top of the steps outside the bulletproof front doors, and gazed at the surrounding buildings and the cars parked in the streets. What Finke told them wasn't a novel idea to him. Cops were targeted all the time by the bad guys who wanted revenge for getting taken down in the past, or pre-emptive strikes in advance of malfeasance.

Somewhere out there in one of those towering buildings, in a room with a window and a view might in fact be someone with a high powered telephoto lens snapping pictures of everyone coming in and out of the building.

Working undercover only functioned while you were invisible, blending in with the crowd. Once you testified in a court of law against a crook, or the bad guys put two and two together and figured out it was you that fingered them, the threat of retaliation increased tenfold.

Unlike a uniformed cop who was out in the open as an enemy combatant, the undercover cop was considered worse than a co-conspirator that turned you in, worse than a relative who ratted you out. The undercover cop to these guys was the lowest of the low. An enemy combatant pretending to be your friend and confidant. Pretending to be one of you. Lying to you. Funny how crooks couldn't stand being lied to. As though they were the only ones allowed that pleasure.

Simon was the last to drive into the parking lot and as he circled around to an open spot and studied the two other men sitting on the bumpers of their respective vehicles, he made up his mind.

"We'll take my car," he said through the rolled down window.

"Why?" asked Poet. He was sitting on the bumper of a mini town car. Fred was sitting on the trunk of an old beat up sedan with tinted windows and faded red paint.

"Isn't it obvious?" said Simon sitting high in the driver's seat of the giant square four door silver SUV with tinted windows. It was the size of a living room with wheels, customized with big knobby tires, oversized struts, stabilizers and shock absorbers.

"We're going to stand out like a sore thumb," said Poet. "If we take my sedan or Fred's piece of junk we'll look like just another couple of dumbasses out for a joy ride. We take this thing and people will be looking at us wondering who we are."

"Isn't that what we're supposed to do?"

"At least you got one thing right," said Fred.

"What's that?" asked Simon.

He pointed to the sticker on the side in big blue letters:

DODGERTOWN.

"See?" said Simon. "He gets it. I put that on the minute I got into this city. I know the score around here. You're either with 'em, or against 'em. Now on the other hand if I put a San Francisco Giants sticker on the side we'd really be looking for trouble. This way we blend right in. We're just some dumbass sports fans out for a joy ride. Plus if anyone decides to go rogue on us, for instance take off on a motorcycle and escape up the side of a mountain we can follow them. With this wheelbase and front end weight we can handle a sixty degree climb. That's one slice of pie less than straight up."

Poet reluctantly locked his car and climbed into the back seat, leaving the front for Fred, their guide. The real reason he didn't want to go with the SUV is he didn't like relinquishing power. Not only was he not driving, but now he was under someone else's control. He had a hard time flying in airplanes because he wasn't the guy doing the actual flying. If something went wrong he was trapped, a prisoner. Simon watched his grumpy facial expression in the rear view and mirror and smiled.

"Don't worry Poet, you can drive anytime you want. It's a blast. Just watch how I run with it and get a feel for the action, how it handles the bumps. Takes a little getting used to, a little bouncy on the highway but it smooths out on the freeways. You just don't want to give it too sharp of a turn when you're going over twenty. It gets a little flippy."

"Oh great," sighed Poet as he settled down into the back seat.

"It took me two years to build it the way I wanted it. It's worth over eighty grand."

He revved the engine a few times as Fred got into the front seat and buckled up. He made the sign of the cross and looked back at Poet with mock fear in his eyes.

A group of pre-teens on skateboards rolled past heading for the mall. As one they all stopped, kicked the tails of their skateboards into their arms and stared at the big black beast. Simon revved the engine a couple of more times and leaned out of the driver's side window.

"You guys stay out of trouble, go to school and get good jobs, and this is you."

Like a boat leaving a safe harbor heading towards the fishing grounds far out in the ocean with no guarantee that they'd catch any fish, or even return to shore they left the parking lot and headed south on the 710, the Long Beach freeway. Traffic was light on a Sunday morning and Simon merged quickly into the fast lane and got up to the speed of the moment at seventy five. The knobby wheels humming and drowning out any normal thinking.

Fifteen minutes later Fred pointed to the right.

"That's Compton."

Simon nodded while keeping his eyes glued to the road, and Poet gazed at the passing scenery. It all looked the same. Low berms on the side of the road, overpasses, glimpses of houses, buildings, billboards. Up ahead was the off ramp to get on the 405 that headed south.

"What do I do here?" asked Simon.

"We don't want the 405. Stay on the 710," said Fred. "It'll take us straight to Long Beach Harbor and then veer to the right and leave us at Terminal Island."

Poet was typing into his phone, pulling up data. Besides busting criminals in the chops the funnest thing in the world for him to do.

"Says here that the 405 freeway is the busiest freeway in the nation. Three hundred seventy five thousand cars a day."

Simon whistled as they passed underneath in the shade of the behemoth. Then the highway curved to the north and they could see ships docked in the harbor. Giant cranes hovering over their hulls. Steel shipping containers hoisted on the ends of cables dangling towards the ground.

Out on the horizon other ships sat seemingly frozen stacked in a line out to sea. Somewhere far over the edge of the sphere hundreds of miles away was a ship with a special cargo.

"Let's go check out contestant number one," said Simon.

Nick Fangano lived on a cul-de-sac a mile from the docks. Tract homes built in the sixties, cracker boxes that sold new for around twenty grand and were now worth close to a million.

"What do we have on him?" asked Fred.

"Thirty eight years old," said Simon. "Married ten years, three kids ages eight to ten."

"Shotgun wedding."

"Gotta be."

"Refinanced the house twice in the past three years, cash out re-fi. Owes more on it now than when he bought it."

"Gotta finance a lavish lifestyle."

"These guys get paid over a hundred grand a year and they can't put money in savings?"

The drove to the next house two blocks over. Same looking house.

"They had five floorplans when they built these homes in 1961," said Simon. "All the same materials, with the same roof lines to save on construction costs, some just a little bigger than the others. They built them like cars on a conveyor belt."

"Craig Balmores, thirty eight, married twenty years straight out of high school, twin boys twenty years old."

"These guys don't wait around do they?"

"Forces of nature."

They drove a few blocks towards town, stopping in front of an apartment complex.

"Jack McDermott. Thirty nine, the old man in the group. Never married. No kids. Rents the apartment. Has a few grand in savings. Goes to Vegas every chance he gets."

"Let's get out of here," said Poet. "We got two weeks to get to know these guys. I'm tired and hungry."

4.

They drove down a narrow block in an old section of the city, following Fred's directions, heading back to the big box and the parking lot with the other two cars.

Tall brownstone buildings separated by dark narrow alleyways with trashcans and trash rolling around in the vee shaped gutters in the middle. The kind of place you wouldn't want to be around in the bottom half of the night. But now in the early morning hour it was quiet, somewhat peaceful.

They passed an adult movie theatre, a pawn shop, a massage parlor, and a liquor store with huddled shapes leaning against the wall outside. Living ghosts getting ready for the night.

"Pull over here," said Fred from the back seat.

"Why? What's going on?" asked Simon as he slowed down and angled into an open spot in between a beat up pickup truck with faded blue paint, a cracked back windshield and bald tires, and a brand new Mercedes with agonizingly crisp silver paint, the surface so perfectly buffed and shiny as though it was covered in liquid mercury.

They all got out of the sedan and looked around, precognizant aware, ready for danger, on the other side of the narrow street was a barber shop and a boxing gym. You could get a haircut and a flattened nose in just a few steps.

Poet was admiring the silver Mercedes parked behind their sedan, he whistled softly, then turned his gaze to the beat up truck.

"Some people might call this diversity, but I say that this is a perfect example of an equal opportunity zone. You have one of the most perfectly maintained cars in the world, and then you have that thing."

"You never can tell," said Fred. "Maybe that truck has a souped up racing engine that could mop up this shiny little foreign car, and the owner purposely keeps it looking like hell so no one will steal it. This is kind of a rough neighborhood if you've noticed."

"Why are we here?" asked Simon.

Fred nodded towards the gym.

"I want you meet my Grandpa."

"How do you know he's here?"

"That's his truck."

He started across the street and they followed. Eleven thirty in the morning and they could hear the steady patter of gloves pelting surfaces. The soft odor of sweating feet and leather wafted from the open double doors which were painted black and covered in flyers.

The interior was brightly lit with fluorescent lighting hanging down from the tall ceiling. In the middle of the large room was a boxing ring raised three feet off the ground with a bouncy floor. Two lightweights were sparring in the center of the ring. Bobbing and weaving while a heavy set man shouted out orders from a chair outside the ring.

Around the edges of the room were weight sets, heavy bags and speed bags. The steady patter that they heard from the outside was a tough looking black man working on the speed bag. Right left right left, over and over, sweat beading on the back of his neck, focused relentless, unyielding, the staccato beat of bag against fist and rim filling the room. Off to the side, sitting in a folding chair while chomping on an unlit cigar was a heavy set man with thin grey hair, like the whisp of a cloud on top of his head, watching the black man on the bag. He looked down at the stop watch in his hand and clicked the top of it.

"Time," he shouted but the black man did not stop, he kept up on the bag, increasing the beat down on the chin of his imaginary enemy until finally when his muscles had reached the end of their capacity, the lactic acid burning the synapses, he finished with one quick knockout right cross and stood there with his gloves on his hips, lungs heaving.

The three detectives approached the man in the folding chair slowly until he turned to watch them in silence.

Fred leaned down and gave him a hug and leaned his forehead in reverence on one of the wide shoulders, then spread his hand and motioned to his compatriots.

"Grandpa, these are my friends, Simon and Poet. The old man nodded and continued chomping on his cigar while studying them, sizing them up.

"Grandpa was one of the top heavyweights a couple of decades ago. Now he's a consultant. A trainer. He had twenty two wins and five losses, and never got knocked out."

The two men nodded with respect.

The minute Simon asked the question he regretted it, but the question slipped out before he could hold it back.

"How'd you do your last fight?"

The old man looked over at Simon, his face gnarled like an old oak tree, eyes steady as though contemplating whether to jump out of the chair and pounce, and yet with all the rough exterior, when he spoke, the words flowed with eloquence.

"I haven't had it yet," said the old man simply while waiting for the reaction in their eyes and facial expressions. "I don't mean I'm going to fight again in the ring," he continued. "And I don't mean I'm going to fight against death. I'm eighty five years old, and no one wins that fight. My last fight, at the very end will be against anger, and remorse. All I want at the end is love and thankfulness for having lived at all. You might think that's unusual for a man who's spent most of his life around a boxing ring filled with actual physical fighting, and bloody vicious brawling for a living. A violent brutal existence, in essence trying to beat the other man's brain in, and knock him unconscious. But you'll see it oftentimes in men who step willingly within the confines of a ring, trapped by four unyielding corners and unmerciful ropes, a trial of physical might. We leave it there, and when we come out from the ropes we live peaceful charitable lives. Oftentimes you have people who have never risked everything, and let it all out within the ring, and yet carry on about their daily lives as though they're in a brawl with the people around them. In my humble opinion they are more dangerous than a trained boxer who has the inner skills necessary for control while in close quarter mortal combat."

The men were all silent as they contemplated what they'd just been told. More as though a diatribe of wisdom, pearls even, from the depths of an ocean of hard fought experience.

Fred smiled and patted his grandfather on the shoulder again.

"Grandpa's also a deacon at our church."

"That was the hardest test of all," said the old man. "To become a Deacon you have to go through a rigorous training regimen somewhat akin to walking your soul across a bed of flaming coals. Unfolding your spirit for all to see, shedding your ego, and walking barefoot across the desert of humanity."

He took out the cigar and smiled. There were a few teeth missing but the grin was as genuine as baby's glee when getting tickled by his mother.

"As you can tell, I have a gift of gab." He winked. "And I'm not afraid to get up in front of hundreds, even thousands of strangers sitting in their pews staring up at me, and tell them a long winded story to enlighten them on the mysteries of heaven and earth. So to answer your question young man, I haven't had my last fight yet. I'm still in training and looking forward to getting in the ring one last time for the ultimate battle that we all must face. Sure we'll all have salvation if we only ask for it with humility and grace, but what is our last thought going to be? That is the most worrisome task ahead of all of us."

"Tell them about your truck Grandpa."

"Looks like a piece of junk, doesn't it?" He waited for a reaction from either Simon or Poet, but Poet merely shrugged.

"Two eighty nine Cobra jet, I can get up to sixty in under four seconds. About a month ago I got it up to a hundred forty on a flat country road outside Redlands."

"One forty?" asked Simon. "Why that's against the law."

Grandpa smiled.

"Not if they don't catch you."

5.

Fred told Simon and Poet that he'd meet up with them at the coffee shop on Lakewood Blvd. around eight thirty the next morning.

"Why eight thirty?" asked Poet.

"I have a meeting every day at seven AM a couple of blocks over on Clark Avenue. It's not a big deal."

"What is it," asked Simon. "AA? I mean it's okay if you go to Alcoholics Anonymous, I know plenty of people it's helped. Usually they meet at seven AM all over the world. Gets 'em prepped for the day. I think it's great actually."

"It's not AA," said Fred.

"Well what is it?" pressed Poet. Now his curiosity was piqued. If Fred had just told them what type of meeting he was going to, it would have been the end of it. But make it a mystery, and now he needed to know.

"Like I said it's not a big deal. I'm a Catholic okay? I've been going to Mass lately, and there's a church a block away that has a Spanish Mass at seven AM. It reminds me of when my

41

Grandma would take me to Mass in the early morning before school."

"You go to Mass every single day?"

"Try to. Like I said it's not a big deal, we'll meet up at eight thirty and then we can head down to the docks and poke around."

Fred had to go to Mass, it had turned into the most important event in his life to start his day. There was no way he was going to miss it.

He went one morning on a whim when he got back into town a few weeks ago, and the place was packed, all the immigrant day workers getting in their faith before heading out to their construction and service jobs.

He sat in the back row in one of the last seats, and then noticed a young woman enter the church looking for a place to sit. He made room right away.

Her head and face were covered by a fine lace veil, and the way she carried herself set off an alarm within him.

Her body language conveyed a sense of humble contrite sorrow, as though out of all the people in the entire church she needed absolution more than any of the others.

Although covered from head to toe in clothes, the way she carried herself, he could sense that she was incredibly beautiful and it was all he could do *not* to look at her, so entranced she was in the service. He didn't want to disturb her peace.

At the end when the Mass ended she left, but gave him just the slightest hint of thanks with sparkling eyes. After that he made sure to attend that same early Mass, and she was there every day to sit next to him. After three weeks of sitting next to each other he finally introduced himself to her and found out her name was Candace. She only gave him her first name, and even though she would not give him her number, or agree to see him outside of the church, not even for coffee, she was there every day sitting inches away.

She seemed to be tired every morning at Mass, and he surmised that she probably worked at night, and ended her day by coming to church. He even considered following her, and using his detective skills to find out everything about her, but he put that thought right out of his mind. That would ruin everything and drive her away. He could tell. Just take your time, he told himself. Even a year if that's what it would take. They had a chemistry, he could feel it, and he knew that she could feel it too.

The Mass this morning was running a little late, the visiting priest was enthusiastic with his homily following the gospel readings, and some of the parishioners were getting anxious, a few left early so they wouldn't be late to work. Bowing their heads low and walking quickly so no one would notice them.

Fred found himself looking at his own watch. Turning his wrist ever so slightly so he could glance at the time. It was eight thirty and he'd be late to the coffee house.

"Have a nice day Candace," he said as they left the pew and headed for the front door.

Her eyes glanced quickly at him, coal black surrounded by absolute beauty. Soft voice like a goddess.

"Thank you Fred. I'll see you tomorrow?"

"Yes, I'll be here early."

And then she was gone, merging with the crowd and heading through the parking lot towards the street. His feet started to follow her, but he forced himself to turn away, just turn away and head to the parking lot to his car.

Getting out of the parking lot at this time of day was hectic, and sometimes a little heated. People were humble in the church, but out in the real world that humbleness turned into 'get out of my way'.

He let a few cars go by and it seemed like it was safe and backed out of his spot.

A car on the other side decided they wanted to get out also and weren't going to wait, and before Fred could react, the other car's rear bumper slammed into his with a crunch of tail lights breaking.

Fred pulled back into his spot while cursing under his breath and got out to check the damage. The other driver left his car where it was in the center of the lane and also got out. He had on dark sunglasses and a black baseball hat pulled backwards on his bald head. Fred held his hands towards his side, palms out.

"I guess you didn't see me."

"You must not have seen *me* asshole," said the man with the black hat. "Now look what you did to my car. You're going to pay for this hombre."

People who were walking to their cars stopped and were watching the commotion, but no one wanted to get involved.

"Look I'm sure we can work this out," said Fred. "I have insurance, let me get my phone and we'll call it in."

He turned and headed back to his car, and that's when the man in the black hat pulled a short barreled pistol from the back of his waistband and shot Fred twice in the back. He slumped to the ground in a heap while the crowd of onlookers scattered under and behind cars.

The man in the black hat walked calmly to his car while still holding the gun at the ready, got into the driver's side, buckled his seatbelt, and drove off through the parking lot and out onto the street, then floored it, tires screeching as he rounded the corner and was gone.

6.

"It's eight thirty, he's late," said Poet as he pushed the plate away from him. Breakfast at the coffee house was a great idea. Eggs and bacon, hash browns, and a slice of hot apple pie to go along with a pot of coffee. He was set for at least half the day.

Simon meanwhile had a bagel with cream cheese and strawberry jam. Fancy boy, thought Poet without saying it out loud. To each his own.

"One thing I dislike," said Simon, "just a tad, is when someone makes an appointment and not only are they late, but they don't have the courtesy to call. My motto is, if you're not early, you're late."

"Maybe the priest had to exorcise the demons and it took him longer than he expected," said Poet. "Oh well, the breakfast was outstanding."

And then they heard the first siren.

"Police," said Poet.

Then they heard another siren, and then another until the air was filled with a dozen wailing sirens of different pitches.

"That's about ten police cars, and two ambulances," said Simon. "Somethings going down in the city."

"And it was such a nice morning," countered Poet as he poured himself another cup of coffee.

At ten minutes to nine they paid their bills and headed to the car.

"Where did he say that church was?" asked Poet.

"Clark Avenue," said Simon as he pulled the map app on his phone, and pointed south west. "Right that way two blocks, where all the sirens were headed a few minutes ago."

Half the parking lot at the church was roped off with yellow tape when they pulled in. Five police cruisers and two black unmarked cars were on the scene, one ambulance. A few dozen civilians were being interviewed by detectives who were busy writing down their report. The witnesses chattering and pointing towards the street. Next to the ambulance which was parked and blocking a couple of cars was a sheet covering what must have been a body.

"What kind of car was Fred driving?" asked Poet.

"The exact same car that's parked right next to that body," said Poet.

Simon pulled in a deep breath and let it out slowly.

"I sure hope our guy is one of the people either taking an interview, or giving one."

"I don't see him anywhere."

"Maybe he's sitting in one of the squad cars, or the ambulance."

They walked towards the police barricade stopping just short of the yellow tape. A thin set officer held up his hand, and stared at them over steel rimmed sunglasses.

"We're looking for our friend," said Simon. "He went to church this morning and was supposed to meet us half an hour ago. That's his car over there."

"Sorry guys, there's been an accident and we're doing an investigation."

"What kind of an accident?"

The officer hesitated, so Poet pulled his wallet out and showed his police ID and badge, then Simon did the same.

"We're cops, on vacation. We're on your side," said Simon. "Our friend's name is Fred Pillar, Filipino guy, twenty eight years old, about five eight, one fifty."

It was subtle, but the officer grimaced, then turned to the crime scene and called out to one of the men in a khaki suit questioning a witness.

"Detective Carter, can you step over here for a moment please."

The man's face was hardened on the edges, eyes inquisitive as he walked over to the yellow tape holding his notepad in one hand and a pen in the other. Simon and Poet showed him their ID's and repeated their story.

"I'm afraid that's your friend under the sheet. He's deceased. Witnesses say there was a fender bender after Mass ended, there was an argument and someone shot your friend twice and raced off."

"I'd like to confirm that," said Poet.

The detective thought for a moment, then held up the tape to let them in and led them to the body, carefully lifted one corner of the sheet so they could see the side of his face. He was still laying on his chest, his hands splayed out as though he were trying to catch himself, bits of gravel sticking to his cheeks. Two dark splotches in between his shoulder blades.

"That's him," said Poet. "He was shot in the back?"

"Yeah," said the detective as he lowered the sheet back in place. "We're waiting for forensics to get here and do a full study of the immediate area, then we'll take him to the morgue for an official ID, and notify his next of kin. How long have you known him?"

"Two days."

"Not long."

"Long enough to want to find the bastard who did this."

That triggered a questioning look from the detective.

"You said you're here on vacation, and been friends for two days?"

Simon was clear and concise, unwavering. He'd interviewed hundreds of suspects over the years, and could spot someone lying with a single look. Finke already supplied them with a convenient alibi if anyone asked, and sure enough here was a time to use it.

"We're here for a convention, a training exercise at the Long Beach Convention Center. Fred was showing us around."

The detective nodded, watching Simon's face

closely.

"Police training exercise?"

Simon nodded.

"Crowd control."

The detective relaxed.

"Yeah, I heard about it. Okay. You said he was supposed to meet you at eight thirty?"

"Yeah, at the waffle house two blocks over. He said he went to church here every morning at seven AM. He called it a meeting. I wonder what he meant by that."

"We talked to a few of the witnesses, some of them recall seeing him here the past few weeks."

"Anyone see the shooter?"

"Most of them were ducking for cover, it's a natural reaction around here. But a couple of them described a thick Spanish or Filipino man dressed all in black, sunglasses, hat, bald head, no identifying tattoos or outstanding features. We're still going to ask them to sit down with our sketch artist."

"What about the car?"

"Nineteen sixty eight standard Camaro coupe, blue, cherry condition, stock everything, but covered in a thick layer of dust."

"Who ID'd the car?"

"That guy right over there." Lieutenant Carter pointed to man standing to the side talking to another suit who was taking notes.

"Mind if I talk to him?" asked Simon.

The lieutenant hesitated for a moment.

"Sure," he said. "Follow me."

The man had tattoos up and down his arm and around his neck, images of saints and skulls and crosses. He stopped talking as they approached.

"These are friends of the victim," said the lieutenant. "This is Carlos. He saw the vehicle leave the parking lot."

"How do you know it was a sixty eight?" asked Simon, getting right to the point.

"I know my cars esse."

"You sure it wasn't a sixty seven, or a sixty nine? The body styles are all the same."

He smiled at that, brilliant white teeth filled here and there with gold.

"But there's a difference, if you know cars."

"The taillights?" pressed Simon.

"Of course. The sixty nine has three taillight lens, while the sixty seven and eight have only two." He waited while his statement sunk in. Trying to see if Simon knew what he was talking about. Testing him.

"Yes," said Simon. "The sixty seven and sixty eight both have two taillights on either side of the rear end. But the standard sixty seven has the white back up light and the red brake light incorporated into one lens, while the sixty eight has the brake light and back up light separated by a bezel. They made one hundred seventy six thousand eight hundred thirteen standard coupes."

Carlos smiled at that.

"That's correct." Then his smile faded as he glanced over at the sheet. "It was a sixty eight, I'm sure of it. There's a few around, but I've never seen that one before. Looked like it was straight up original. Like it was never even driven. Sounded smooth as silk but a little rough on the idle, like it hadn't been serviced in a while. But even with the coat of dust I could tell it was in mint condition."

"You said it was blue."

"Yeah."

"What tint, there's a few different ones you know."

"Yeah esse, it was color code KK."

Carlos watched Simon's eyes, testing him again. He seemed to take pleasure in the challenge.

"Tripoli turquoise," said Simon. "I love that color, kind of edging towards grey."

"We use it in our shop now and then. It's a Chevy original."

"You know your stuff," said Simon. "Thank you."

The man reached into his wallet and pulled out a card and handed one to Simon.

"You know your stuff too, if you ever need any work done give us a call. Or maybe I could even put *you* to work."

"Anything else you can think of?" asked Simon. "Did anyone here know our friend?"

Carlos nodded. "There was a girl that he sat with every morning at the back of the church. She wore a veil so you couldn't really see her face, but you could tell by the way that she moved that she was fine tuned. She has a golden Aztec moon tattoo on her left ankle."

"You noticed the tattoo on her ankle?" asked Simon.

Carlos nodded.

"Beautiful cars, beautiful women. The best things in life esse."

He looked over at the sheet again, and made the sign of the cross.

He thought twice, then gave a card to the lieutenant, and walked over to a young woman who was waiting off to the side.

"We've got an all points out for that car," said Carter. "Sounds like it's unusual enough and should stand out like a sore thumb. Good work with your interview. Color code KK. Tripoli turquoise Who would have known. And the woman with the tattoo, we'll follow up on that one too."

A three man team in an unmarked black car with tinted windows pulled into the parking lot.

"Forensics," said Carter. He gave Simon a business card with his contact info on it. "You can stay here as long as you want and accompany the body if you'd like, but let's make sure to connect later. We just got word of a bank robbery. It's going to be a busy day."

They watched as the team walked straight to the body, carefully pulled the sheet off and started photographing and searching the area for evidence. One man picked up the two bullet jackets and put them in a plastic bag.

"Let's get out of here, we're wasting time," said Poet. He'd been silent the whole time, listening, observing, taking in the whole scene, from the church front door to every edge of the parking lot, the faces of all the people still present, the still sheet covering the body, the description of the car.

Simon nodded and they walked back to the edge of the lot.

"Change of plans," said Simon.

"Yeah," said Poet. "That little drug deal down at the docks is gonna have to wait. I don't care how long I knew Fred. He was my partner, and no one guns down my partner and gets away with it."

"Agreed," said Simon.

They were silent as they walked back to the car, shoes crunching on light gravel.

"I'll drive," said Poet, and Simon didn't argue as they got in the sedan.

"We only knew Fred for a couple of days," said Simon. "But I'll be damned it sure seems longer. Funny how that happens. You meet a guy's grandpa and suddenly it's like you're part of the family. It's a hell of a job we have here. I've only been in this line of work for ten years, and I've seen two dozen uniforms hung up forever. Old guys, young guys, one young woman, all with families. You know we're going to have to go back and see his grandpa. But I don't want to do that until we have the guy who did it behind bars."

"Or dead," finished Poet. "Shot Fred in the back. Damn coward."

"Something's a little fishy here," said Simon. "A car in mint condition, covered in dust. A little fender bender and he shoots our buddy."

"In the back," reiterated Poet. "Now how in the hell did that happen? How could it happen? Fred was a ring tested boxer, he would never turn his back on someone if he felt he was in danger."

"Maybe he saw the gun and tried to run away."

"Naw, that doesn't fit. I don't even think he knew the guy had a gun."

Simon turned on the police scanner while Poet drove. Dispatch was directing patrols to different locations.

There was the bank robbery and the pursuit through the streets of L.A. An assault on Hollywood and Vine. Domestic disturbance at an apartment complex. Drunk driver crashed his car into a mailbox, and it wasn't even lunchtime yet. A lady complaining about barking dogs. It was a busy morning.

Then they heard a call that caught their attention.

"Car on fire underpass of the 405 freeway. Near the Baker Street Park, next to the Los Angeles River."

Simon looked up the location on the satellite map. "Just south of Cerritos. Twenty minutes away."

By the time they got there the fire was out and the fire truck was wrapping up their gear and getting ready to head out again. A single cop was photographing the heap of twisted metal and poking around the ruins for evidence.

Someone crashed through a chain link fence and burned the car in an empty dirt field next to the freeway overpass.

What was left of the it was a blackened heap that looked like it got caught in a war zone and torn apart by a missile, the gas tank must have exploded and ripped the frame in half. The hood was twenty feet away, upside down and like the rest of the car that it had been ejected from, was covered in foam from the firefighters.

They parked at the end of Baker street and waited until everyone left. No sense in bringing attention to themselves. First the fire engine roared to life and plodded off, then the cop got in his car, said something into the mic and followed.

They left their car where it was and walked through the hole in the fence to the wreck.

"Some kids having fun?"

"Someone trying to get rid of the evidence," said Simon. "It's a Camaro."

"How can you tell?"

"Some of the shape is still there. Check out the hood sitting there all by itself upside down, it must have been ejected by the explosion, semi intact, and while the rest of the car's body burned and melted, it sat over there with a little bit of flame around it, melting the paint, but the shape is intact."

They walked over and Simon bent down and touched the cross bar on the bottom of the hood to make sure it was cooled down.

He lifted the hood and flopped it over so they could inspect the top. Burnt and blackened soot covered it. He took a small knife out of his pocket and scrapped off some of the soot until the slight hint of blue showed through.

"Tripoli turquoise."

He pointed at the car behind them.

"We need a VIN number."

They walked back over to the hulk. The smell of burnt rubber and metal overwhelmed them.

When the gas tank exploded it buckled the car in two, ejecting the hood, breaking all the windows and melting all the hoses, seats and plastic parts.

"If this is an original vehicle like Carlos said, then there should be a vehicle identification number stamped on a little metal plate under the front drivers side of the windshield." Then Simon shook his head as they got closer to the car and looked closely at the spot where it should be.

"Should be right there. Why am I not surprised it's gone. Either someone removed it before setting it on fire, or it got ejected with the explosion. I'm betting it was removed. But the good news is there's two hidden VIN for these Camaros. One is under the passenger side cowl which is gone, and the other is on the firewall behind the heater blower box."

Simon went to the other side of the car and used a flashlight to peer down at the firewall, with the hood gone and most of the engine including the heater box blown away, he had a clear shot, then spit on his fingers and reached down into the opening to rub the metal, feeling for the VIN tag.

"Here it is."

He took out his phone, set the camera for flash then maneuvered it into the opening and took a couple of photos. The numbers were blackened but stood out enough with the flash to be readable.

124378N501027.

"That's a lot of numbers," said Poet.

Simon pulled up a database on his phone to decipher the numbers.

"It's a sixty eight two door coupe with a V-8 engine and was built in the Norwood, Ohio factory. Twelve means it's a Camaro, four means an eight cylinder, thirty seven means it's a two door coupe, eight means it was built in sixty eight, and the N means it was built in the Norwood, Ohio factory. The last six digits are the assembly line number and for that we need access to the DMV. Hopefully it's registered here in California. Last I checked there were fifteen million cars registered in this state."

In the shadows of the overpass they sensed movement. In one corner of the shadows a shabby dressed man pushing a shopping cart filled with big plastic bags, clothes, empty bottles. In another corner a woman sat with her dog, rocking back and forth to an invisible tune.

"You know," said Poet. "The funny thing about a spot like this, even secluded as it is, a godforsaken little hole under the freeway. Someone saw the person, or people who lit this car on fire. There's a witness."

Simon shook his head. "No one that's going to be any use to us."

Poet nodded in agreement.

"The other interesting angle is that there's no houses or businesses out here. No security cameras to video tape the perp."

"Yeah. Pretty obvious whoever did this had it all figured out well ahead of time. This wasn't a crime of instant passion. A little fender bender during rush hour in the middle of a parking lot at a church with a lot of witnesses. Destroying the getaway vehicle in a place that no one cares about. Seems like the cop that was investigating this little fire couldn't get out of here quick enough. A couple of photos for the report and onto the next one."

"Think we should call Lieutenant Finke and let him know what we found out?"

"And get caught up in their red tape? Let those guys in homicide put this lead into a pile next to another pile and get to it when they can? Look around, we're the only ones here."

"I was testing you."

"Well don't do it again."

"Run the number."

Simon pulled out the cheat sheet with the access codes, then punched the keyboard.

"California DMV. We're in."

He punched in the thirteen digits.

"Clement Sinclair Gardinar. Isn't that an unusual name."

"Yeah, it's an old style name. The kind they used back in the turn of the century." He rolled the name over and over. "Seem like I've heard it before." He punched the first name in a search engine. Up popped the origin of the name and a list of famous people. "It's a French surname. Most of the people on this list were born in the first few decades of the last century. Here's one, Clement Freud, the grandson of Sigmund Freud, born 1924, died 2009."

""Forget about that guy. We just want the guy

who owns the car."

"Get this, last registered here in the great state of California in nineteen seventy five. This car hasn't been registered to drive for fifty years. And the address on record is in Wichita, Kansas."

"He must have moved the car here from Kansas."

"Check the state tax database."

"Yeah, here he is. Clement S. Gardinar. Born in 1935. He's ninety years old. Twenty two fifty nine Sicamore Avenue. Reseda."

7.

The house was set back from the street in the old section of East L.A.

They didn't build neighborhoods like this anymore, with space between the houses, the structures set back from the street. The streets themselves were wide and more likely referred to as a boulevard, or an avenue. Stately mansions belonged on streets like these, yet harbored small old houses built just before the prior century.

Giant walnut, and sycamore trees shaded the sidewalks while their giant deep roots cracked and lifted the concrete walkway that meandered down the boulevard. Step on a crack and break your mommas back was not the saying heard on this street. It was step on a crack and break your own back. You could hide a small animal within some of the cracks of the ruffled walkway. Children, if there were any nearby, could play hide and seek in the crevice's.

Poet parked the sedan close to the curb next to one particularly gnarled slab, and when

Simon tried to open the passenger door he was stymied, the bottom edge meeting sharp tilted concrete.

"You mind moving up a notch so I can get out?" asked Simon politely. "Man, we need a bigger car. I feel like a sardine in a can."

Poet however was studying the house and the empty driveway leading up to it. The pattern of leaves piled high at the entrance.

"Doesn't look like anyone's been here in a while. No tire tracks in the carpet of leaves. None broken or smashed."

"What are you an Indian tracker? Move up a bit so I can get out."

Poet, taken out of his observant trance started the car and moved forward past the driveway to a semi-flat section of sidewalk, parking far enough away from the curb, and they both got out and looked around the neighborhood. The street was fairly quiet with two spots of activity. A landscape company three doors down was busy mowing, weed whacking and blowing leaves into big piles, while a few doors down from them an old lady was walking a dog across the street. Other than that the block of old houses was empty. Guaranteed there were eyes watching them from nearby windows.

They walked through the carpet of leaves, up the steps to the front door, Poet reaching over and pushing the doorbell, while Simon watched the window to the side. They could hear the TV blaring a news channel. A talking head detailing some disaster or another for a dulled audience.

Poet rang the doorbell again, then knocked

on the door. The intercom below the doorbell came to life, a scratchy voice asking who was there.

Poet leaned down and spoke clearly into the device so the occupant, and anyone else within earshot could hear.

"We're the police Mr. Gardinar. Just here to ask you a few questions if you can spare the time."

The voice on the other end wheezed lightly and then rasped.

"The door is open."

Simon reached out and turned the knob and opened the heavy door. The living room was overall dark with the tint of blue television light glowing on the walls. But the first and overwhelming sense that hit them was the distinct order of what can only be described as old person smell. An invisible toxic cloud that spilled out of the door.

"Aldehyde," said Simon.

"What the hell is that?" whispered Poet, his face scrunched into a ball, hesitant to move forward beyond the threshold.

"When you remove hydrogen from alcohol you get formaldehyde, otherwise known as aldehyde. It's a natural process with humans as they age."

"That about sums up what I'm smelling," whispered Poet. "That and dried urine. Otherwise known as piss."

"He's ninety eight years old," said Simon. "I don't think you need to whisper." He pushed the door completely open and stepped inside, ushering Poet into the house and closing the door behind them.

Hunched in a wheelchair, clear tubes leading from an oxygen tank to nostrils sat a frail old man. His shoulders covered in a tattered blanket. The TV was situated to the left end of the room and he had the wheelchair angled to he could both watch it and the door. The TV sound was turned up to an obnoxious level.

"You're not Wade," rasped the old man.

"No we're not," said Simon. "We're with the police. We'd like to ask you a couple of questions if that's okay."

"But where's Wade?"

"You mind if we turn the sound on the TV down a bit?"

Not waiting for a reply, Simon reached slowly for the channel changer on the small table next to the wheel chair and muted the volume. Now they could all think and converse clearly.

Poet moved closer to the old man so he could lean over and ask him a question.

"Who's Wade?"

The old man's eyes widened as his vision focused on the sudden large black man looming in front of him.

"Please don't hurt me," wheezed the old man instinctively. There was no sense of play acting in the old man's reaction. For whatever reason he was terrified.

Poet took a step back and diminished his frame, pulling his shoulders together, lowering his chin onto his chest, becoming non-threatening, placing his hands folded in front of him as though he were here to serve. No sense in arguing with the old geezer. He was suddenly afraid, and that was a reaction that needed to be respected in his own house.

Simon pulled out his badge and ID, slowly and methodically holding them close to the old man.

"We're cops, Mr. Gardiner. Just here to ask you a couple questions about a car."

The old man's eyes seemed to light up. A spark of life behind the watery grey iris's.

"What car?"

"A nineteen sixty eight Camaro."

He tilted his head in thought.

"Yes, I have one in the garage. I have five cars left." His voice trailed off. "They're all I have left."

"Can we take a look at it?"

He feebly waved a wrinkled hand.

"Yes, the doors open."

Simon stood straight and motioned with his head to Poet to check it out.

"I'll stay here with Mr. Gardiner."

Poet nodded and headed for the front door, grateful to be leaving the living morgue.

Simon pulled a flat backed chair closer to the wheelchair and smiled at the old man who has fallen asleep. Or maybe has just closed his eyes to rest them.

"So who's Wade?"

The watery eyes opened as the thought came to life, and the old man appeared to be lucid for a short moment.

"Wade Shelding is my nurse and cook. He

comes once a day to prepare two meals, and help me clean up." His eyes trailed off. It was obvious what he meant by clean up a bit. It didn't look like the old man could raise up out of the wheel chair on his own, let alone sit on a porcelain throne without assistance.

"Is it possible that he was here already today?"

"I...don't...know..." the old voice rasped. His eyes closed slowly. A light whistling sound came from the oxygen tubes in front of his nostrils with each short breath. He was asleep.

Simon got up and walked around the living room. Every surface was covered in varying layers of dust. A plate of half-eaten food, mashed potatoes, boiled vegetables and some type of ground up meat was on the floor next to the wheel chair and crawling with ants. Magazines and newspapers piled in corners and lining the walls around the room. It was a bit of a pigsty and Simon felt remorse for the old man to be living in this condition.

If you could even call what he was doing living.

He went through the kitchen to the back door and out to the garage, a large structure with three garage doors, nearly the size of a house under a giant peach tree.

Rotten fruit covered the tin roof, and what had once been a concrete driveway. One of the garage doors was open and he could see Poet inside, inspecting the cars.

There were four of them. Like the interior of the living room, each of them covered in a fine layer of dust. It was hard to tell what color they were.

"The old man said there were five," said Simon as he walked into the shadow of the garage.

"The light doesn't work, bulb must be burnt out," said Poet. "But as you can see, there's only four cars here, and no Camaro."

The four cars were parked in two rows, front bumper to rear bumper in two of the bays, while the third bay was empty and there was a shadow, like an outline on the floor where the dust was less than the surrounding area.

"About the size of a Camaro wouldn't you say?" said Poet.

They walked closer to the cars. Poet reached out a finger and traced it along one of the hoods. It was silver.

"This is a Bentley, the one in front is a Rolls Royce. The other two look like a Mustang and maybe a Ferrari."

"Not a Ferrari," countered Simon. "It's a Bugatti. Probably a fifty eight. Their designs crossed paths for a couple of years in the late fifties. Quite an eclectic choice of collectables. Did you notice the peaches lining the driveway outside."

"How could I miss them? I should have worn my boots this morning."

Simon reached up and unlatched the lever for the garage door in the third empty bay and lifted the door, sliding it up over his head. There, in the layer of disintegrated fruit were two tire tracks leaving the garage straight down the drive way.

"Notice how the tracks are still evident in the rotten fruit," said Simon, "but the other half of the driveway leading down to the street has a fresh layer of leaves covering whatever tracks might be there. Those new leaves could have fallen overnight. What do you think the chances are," he wondered, "that the old man took a joy ride in the Camaro and forgot where he left it?"

"That poor old pile of racist bones can't even get out of his wheel chair to go wee-wee. I think the chances are higher that our missing man Wade stole the old man's car. Did you notice how filthy that house was in there? That's a crime in itself. Doesn't take a trained detective to see that something's wrong here."

"Think we should visit some of the neighbors and see if they know anything?"

"I think we should call protective services and give them a tip to come get that old guy. He looks like he's ready to croak any minute. Did you see the way he reacted when he saw me just standing there? I might have given him a heart attack right then and there just from the color of my skin."

"Maybe it was your breath."

Simon pulled a small plastic box from his pocket, shook it, and handed it towards Poet.

"Breath mint?"

Poet's eyes narrowed, his fist clenching, then relaxed.

"Sure, maybe it will take away some of the lovely smells that abound this residence."

He took two mints, popped them in his

mouth and handed the box back to Simon.

Poet closed the garage doors while Simon went back into the house to check on Mr. Gardiner who was still sleeping and snoring slightly, then used the old man's cell phone to call protective services and ask for a courtesy visit. They wanted all kinds of details, but he cut them short and said it was borderline an emergency, repeated the address and hung up.

He pulled up the list of recent calls, took a screen shot with his own phone and closed the door gently behind him.

Poet was standing next to the car waiting.

Off in the distance they could hear the faint whine of a siren. It wasn't fire or ambulance, it was the police.

"You better hurry if you don't want to explain why you're here."

"Running from the law at my age," said Poet, shaking his head as he scrunched his large frame into the driver's seat and pushed it back a few notches.

While they drove away from the house, Simon pulled up his tracking website and punched in the numbers on the screenshot.

There were only three different numbers for the past few months, one was a doctor's office with multiple calls back and forth, one was a telemarketer that called him once, and one was a Wade Shelding who called multiple times over the past few months, the last call was two days ago and lasted twenty seconds.

He pulled up the data sheet on Wade. Forty eight years old. Single. Did not own property.

Had a nineteen ninety eight Chevy Blazer.

Renting an apartment in Reseda, and had a long list of criminal convictions, twenty eight in all   mostly drug and traffic. The last one resulting in a three year prison term that he finished serving a year ago.

And then another citation for driving without a license last month. No theft or violence. Yet even now, forty eight years of age, old enough to know better and still getting into trouble.

8.

Within an hour they pulled up in front of the apartment building in Reseda. Brown stucco, three story with balconies on the fronts and sides. The sun was setting, the sky rusty orange in the west, street lights slowly gaining strength to match the coming darkness, although in the sprawl of the city of the angels it was never completely dark and no one would be watching the stars tonight or any other night.

No one was home in the apartment on the second floor, or at least no one answered the door when they knocked. While Poet blocked the view of the door with his frame, widening his elbows at his sides and squatting slightly, Simon jimmied the door open with the crowbar and they were in. The place was indeed empty, and was nearly the squalor that they'd just left on the other side of town.

Dirty floors and dirty dishes piled high in the sink. The stink was not as bad as the old man's house but had a different aroma, more like dried sweat caked on cloth surfaces.

"Gimme a few of those breath mints," said Poet. "I hope you're carrying a good supply."

Simon shook the box and handed it to him.

"You keep it, I've got a backup."

Poet popped two in his mouth, then thought better of it and took an extra one.

"So maybe it wasn't criminal intent, this Wade dude taking such poor care of that old man. This is how he lives in real life. Same kind of filth and grime, just maybe a little less dust."

"The report I got said he's only lived here two months," said Simon, "give it some time."

"I'll give it about two hours and then I say we go looking for this bum somewhere else."

"You can wait in the car if you want. I'll call you if he comes home."

"And let you have all the fun? Not a chance."

Three hours later they were still waiting in the dark. Poet sat on the floor near the door, since it was about the cleanest place in the apartment, while Simon stood leaning against the glass slider watching the alley below. People milling about, small clusters of lost souls up to no good. Shuffling their feet.

The doorknob rattled. A voice on the other side semi incoherent.

"What the hell... someone broke my door. Damn man..."

The door opened a crack revealing a disheveled man with a half beard clutching a brown paper bag to his chest, the hallway light illuminating the interior of the apartment. Poet reached out and grabbed the man with one hand at the back of his neck, pulled him through the door and flew him into the living room where Simon was waiting with zip ties for the feet and hands. The man was hogtied before he stopped rolling. He lay on his back, eyes wide, took a deep breath and looked like he was about to shout when Poet put his big foot right on top of the open lips stymying any outburst.

"This how you like to live? This whole place is like the bottom of my dirty shoe. In fact, I'd say the bottom of my dirty shoe is cleaner than any surface in this filthy damn apartment, so you must be feeling right at home with my heel on your tongue. Now if I take my foot offa your mouth will you promise not to yell out?"

The man was struggling to breath and nodded his head feverishly.

"Okay then," said Poet as he pulled his foot up and then stood to the side towering over the man who first spat out to the side and then gasped for breath.

"I didn't do it, I promise," he whispered with wild eyes.

"Didn't do what?" asked Simon, joining the party again from the other side.

"Whatever it is you think I did. You're cops right?"

"What makes you think we're cops?" said Poet.

"You look like cops, you smell like cops. You don't act like cops but I can spot a cop a mile away."

Simon leaned down and placed his hand on the man's chest.

"Well guess what Wade, you're right, we are

cops, but unfortunately for you we're the bad kind. The kind that don't take you to the precinct for questioning. That's a little too fancy for us. We like to work a little different. We get the answers that we need without reading you the Miranda rights. Those pesky little details get in the way. Take too much time."

Poet leaned down and wrapped his hand around the man's wrist that was lashed tight to his left.

"I'm a little grumpy right now from spending the past three hours in this dump waiting for you to show up, and I ran out of breath mints half an hour ago, so don't give me no run around. Our friend was shot in the back this morning and we think you did it."

A sudden chill went through Wades body and he went limp. Sweat appeared on his forehead, first a mist of perspiration, then beads the size of sand pebbles. He tried to speak, but words failed to pass through his voice box.

"There's a car," said Simon. "A Camaro that was used in the crime."

Wade's eyes widened as he realized the implication.

"We went to the old man's house today," said Poet. "The car was missing and so were you. It's a shame the way you mistreated that poor old man and forcing him to live in squalor like yourself. But it's even more of a shame that you took his car and then shot our friend in the parking lot of the church this morning after he said his prayers in Mass. It might be about time for you to say your own prayers."

In some ways, a wave of relief passed through Wade as he realized the mistake that these men were making in their assumptions. He was quick with an answer. Thinking of an alibi while getting grilled by the cops was his specialty. It didn't work every time, but what they couldn't prove couldn't hurt you, and in this case he was in the clear.

"I didn't do it," he blurted. "Absolutely one hundred percent I did not have anything to do with anyone getting shot this morning." He nodded his head in finality.

"But you took the car," said Poet, while increasing his grip on Wade's wrist.

He thought hard before answering but there was probably no getting out of that one. Maybe one of the neighbors saw him drive off, even though it was night. He gritted his teeth. Then it came to him.

"Well, yeah I borrowed the car. Mr. Gardiner said I could borrow any of the cars whenever I wanted." He breathed a sigh of relief, believing that his statement could never be disproven.

"You borrowed it."

"Yup."

Poet shook his head, dreadfully disappointed.

"You see Wade, the term borrow is from the Middle English 'borowen' used in jolly old England about a thousand years ago. It even has some origin from Old German, Saxon, the word 'borg' to pledge or protect. It's an adjective meaning to lend for a time, it's an action phrase. The word 'borrower' however is a noun, you being the borrower and a physical being. The word itself implies that at some point in time you return the item that you borrowed. But you didn't return the car, did you?"

A light blinked in Wade's mind. He had the answer.

"No I didn't. I tried to, but the dang car broke down. It's almost a hundred years old."

"It's a '68 Camaro Wade. It's only fifty three years old."

"Might as well be a hundred. It's old. It broke down on Crenshaw, by the park and ride. I left it and went to get a mechanic to help me and when I got back it was gone."

"What's the mechanic's name?"

"John Montgomery."

"You got a phone number?"

"Oh man...I got it off an ad on a bus stop bench."

"You ever hear the term bald face liar?"

Wade shook his head, out of answers.

"Shakespeare coined part of the term, 'beardless, with no hair upon the face'. In time it came to mean bold, shameless, as a young impudent boy. Then Harriet Beecher Stowe referenced a barefaced lie in Uncle Tom's Cabin which happens to be one of my favorite books. You sir, even though you have a scraggly beard, are a bare faced liar. Now you want to tell me what you did with the car?"

"I already told you, it broke..."

At the word broke, Poet grabbed Wade's thumb with his right hand while still grasping his wrist with his left and with a quick twist popped the thumb out of the socket. The sound was like a chicken bone snapped in two, the thumb now pointing at an odd angle straight down along the arm instead of up and aligned with the other fingers, some of the bone itself poking through the skin, blood flowing down the side.

Simon had reached over and pressed his hand firmly over Wade's mouth with all his weight behind it, muffling the scream.

Wade's body shook uncontrollably for a few moments then went still as shock began to set in. His eyes were still open, and fully intent on Poet who still had his wrist and hand in a vice grip.

"One down," said Poet. "Nine to go. You want to tell me now where you left the car?"

"Don't forget he's got toes too," said Simon.

"What?" asked Poet.

"Nine more fingers and ten more toes. That's nineteen more appendages you can snap."

Keeping his grip on the wrist with his left hand, Poet moved his right hand over and wrapped it around the index finger.

"Okay, okay!" Wade whispered.

Nothing was worth this amount of pain, he thought. I'll leave the city, they'll never find me. I'll tell these guys the truth, and they can deal with it.

"His name's Leo."

"Leo what?"

"Leo Andrade." He caught his breath and squeezed tears out his eyes. It was too late to back out now, it was over. "They call him the lion. I owed him money and gave him the car. I didn't think the old man... Mr. Gardiner would even miss the car. He's almost dead. I didn't have anything to do with anyone getting shot I swear to God. But Leo... I don't know... He's a killer. And I'm getting out of this city tonight and never coming back."

"Okay," said Poet. "Alright. I've been in this business long enough to know when someone's finally telling the truth. I believe you. And now I'm going to do you a favor."

Simon reached over and put all his weight on his hand that was over Wade's mouth while Poet popped the thumb back in place, the cracking sound less severe now but still loud. Wade's scream muffled as he shook in pain, then he was still, sobbing, pulling short tearful breaths into his flaring nostrils.

Simon took the Glock from the holster under his armpit and prodded Wade under the chin with the barrel. Pressing it into the bone.

"Don't make us come looking for you again."

Then he rebolstered the gun, pulled a switchblade from his pocket and cut the zip ties.

"Where's your phone?" asked Poet.

Wade thought about sitting up, then reconsidered and stayed on his back.

"In my front pocket."

"Pull it out and unlock it."

The man did as he was told, and Simon punched his finger on the recent call list and took a picture with his own phone of the numbers.

"Which one is Leo's number?"

"The last one on the list. He keeps calling me

and calling me."

"Why don't you answer?" asked Poet mercilessly.

Wade got quiet, eyes trembling, breath slow and silent, unable to respond to the question.

Simon threw the phone on the ground and walked out followed by Poet.

9.

"Leo the lion," said Poet as he drove the car down the street. "Sounds like a real tough guy."

"Sounds like a character from a comic book," countered Simon as he opened up his laptop and punched the number into the data base. "It's a burner phone. No address associated with this device."

"How long's he owned it?"

"One month."

"Yeah, it's a burner. Give him a call. Maybe he'll meet up with us. Tell him we're looking to bet some big money, or buy some drugs."

"Crazy. Sure that'll work."

Simon reached into the back of the car and pulled out his backpack, taking out a square rectangular box the size of a loaf of bread.

"What's that?"

"You never seen one of these? It's a Stingray."

"I've heard about them. Aren't they illegal to use without a warrant?"

Simon smiled. "Imagine that. Why yes Poetamos, technically I guess they are illegal.

But I'm not exactly a technical or a legal kind of guy right now. I'm the kind of guy that wants to find the bastard who shot my partner in the back kind of guy no matter what it takes."

He hooked up a short black antenna to the back of the box with a long wire. The antenna had a suction cup with a lever on the bottom of it. Simon rolled down the window, reached out and put the suction cup on the back corner of the hood of the car and winched down the lever, squeezing all the air out of the cup and cementing the antennae onto the metal.

"You sure that thing aint gonna blow off?"

"Tested to a hundred mile per hour wind. You planning on going that fast?"

"Not likely in this town with all the traffic."

Simon powered up the device and used a USB line to hook it to his laptop. A software program loaded an interface onto the screen.

"We're in business." He looked at the screenshot of Wade's phone and punched Leo's phone number into the interface. A little circle rotated on the screen, the device was searching for the phone.

"You see the way it works, this device acts like a cell phone tower. Every cell phone in the world constantly searches for and hooks up to the most powerful tower in the vicinity. This device is more powerful than any tower and overpowers them. Not only do we have access to the target phone, but all the other phones in the area. Right now I have ten thousand phones hooked in. But I'm only looking for one."

"Does he have to be using his phone, or does

it have to be turned on? What if he has it turned off?"

"Yes, the phone does have to be turned on. But he doesn't have to be using it. That's the beauty of it. You see the cell phone is really just a glorified walkie talkie. It sends out radio signals that are intercepted by a cell tower and then relayed to the phone on the other end. Even when the phone isn't being used, it's configured to continually find the best tower for when that call does get made."

"How'd you get that thing?"

"I know a guy."

"You know a guy huh?"

"Yeah, it pays to have connections. This little box retails for around fifty grand. I'm just borrowing it."

"Well don't break it then. Usually when I borrow things I end up breaking them. Bikes, cars, fishing poles, people."

"You broke a person?"

"Yeah, one time I was painting our house and there was a little spot up high that I couldn't get to on my little ladder. The neighbor next door had a guy mowing his lawn and he was really tall. I asked if I could borrow him for a couple of minutes so he could reach up and paint the little spot. He said no problem, the lawn guy said no problem, so he gets up on the ladder and reaches up with paint brush."

"Don't tell me. He fell off the ladder and broke his arm."

Poet shook his head.

"He fell off the ladder and broke both his

arms. That was a problem."

'Well then keep your hands off this Stingray device. I don't want to have to pay back fifty grand."

"Damn expensive toy."

"It's a cheap one too."

"Fifty grand gets you a cheap one?"

"It's a year old. You know how that goes with electronics."

"Does it even work?"

"One way to find out. You see first we need to reverse engineer the phone number to find the IMSI, the international mobile subscriber identity number. Then the stingray identifies that signal, separates it from all the rest of the signals, then measures it's distance and direction. As we drive around the distance and direction changes. We are in essence triangulating the phones location."

"What if he's driving around also?"

"Doesn't matter. The device is calculating thousands of measurements per second."

"Anything yet?"

"Nothing. Take a left up here."

"Turning left on Sunset."

Traffic was flowing smooth. Red tail lights in front of them streaming straight off into the distance, white headlights coming from the other direction.

"A lot of cars on the road," said Poet. "Friday night."

Both men were silent for a few moments as one watched the road, while the other watched the computer screen with numbers streaming across the face.

"Bingo," said Simon finally. "General location is northwest two miles. Take the next right, and then the next left and we should have it."

The satellite map showed a large circle encompassing a few city blocks, then as they drove forward zig zagging through the streets, and as the software computed the changing distance and direction, the circle got smaller and smaller until it was a tiny red dot. Simon zoomed in on the street.

"Mei Rose Place," he said. "Stay on this street for the next half mile then turn left on Rosencrans and right on Mei Rose."

They pulled up in front a row of brown stucco apartments. There was a liquor store on the corner and a laundromat next to it. Full bodied shadows, people standing next to a brick wall that bordered an alleyway next to the liquor store, their shapes barely noticeable in the dark night air, only distinguishable now and then with the occasional puff of white smoke billowing from their mouths, cigarettes or worse.

Poet turned off the engine, holstered his pistol in his armpit sling and got ready to get out of the car.

"Son of a bitch," said Simon.

"Now what?"

"The red dot disappeared. It's dead."

"There's probably a hundred apartments on this street," said Poet. "He killed the phone?"

"He's here somewhere, we'll wait and watch."

10.

"C'mon baby take it all off!"

"Show your tits!"

"Come over here and sit on my face!"

Rude comments weren't the norm, but what else could you expect with a mixture of alcohol, horny men and hot oiled women stripping off their clothes and dancing a few inches from their eyes.

You were inviting it.

In a way it was a competition between the strippers to see who could make the animals throw more of their money at them.

Subtle provocative flirting usually did the trick. Eyes and lips and curves, and places on a woman that they normally would never see unless in a place like this.

Grinding rock music, glaring colored lights, a savage thumping edge to the vibe. Bordering on primeval animals dancing around the fire after a successful hunt.

It was both dangerous and safe at the same time. You weren't supposed to see things like this, but yet here you could sit in a legal environment watching live women take off every bit of clothing. Not a still shot from a magazine but vibrant pulsing flesh. The only thing you couldn't do is touch, and there were tough men on the watch to protect the assets of the club. Reach out and touch and get put in a headlock and thrown out the door.

Candace Fernandez, twenty four years old, sweet, innocent demeanor with big brown eyes, jet black hair, soft luxurious tan skin, and a body that made men melt in the seats. Her stage name was Candy and at Dreamers, the club that she danced at, the decibel volume of cheers went up a few notches when she went on stage. So angled and perfect were her curves that even the women in the audience stopped talking and took note.

Every half hour, for five minutes she had a turn on stage. She came out in a tight fitting white skirt with lingerie underneath, and when she left it was all draped over her shoulders.

Liquor sales seemed to stop when she came on stage and the waitresses took a break, not because it was a rule, it was just that every eyeball in the place was fixated on a five foot two bombshell that demanded attention.

With every bump and grind and luscious wanton looks at the patrons surrounding the stage, money flew at her feet. Men begged her to take bills from their hands so they could get closer to her.

What no one in the entire place knew however, and no one would ever know, is that she hated every moment with her skin bared for all to see, but at the same time it wasn't the worst thing in life, not by far, but it was a necessary event in her daily routine, a hurdle in the road of life that she travelled every day.

She needed the money more that anyone of them, more than any of the patrons, or fellow workers, and so she developed a technique to overcome her complete and utter aversion. A mental blockade. A completely impenetrable psychological barrier. She called it the pit, and when she walked in through the back door of the club, past the dumpster and the grease trap, past the recycled bottles, cans, and empty kegs, she transformed herself completely, converting first her mind, and then her body from Candace innocent civilian pure as the driven snow, to Candy, the most incredible enchantress the world has ever seen.

During the conversion at the back door she said a short quiet prayer and nestled her spirit in a safe place, until it could be retrieved and revived. Nothing could harm her, nothing could change her faith. Seven hours in the pit. Fourteen five minute shifts on the stage and she was done. Seventy minutes in total of living a lie and she could walk with a wad of cash.

Four thirty in the morning and her shift was over, and yet the leering faces and voices from strangers lingered in her mind.

She shook it off and counted her tips in silence.

Five girls in all sat in the cramped dressing room taking off their makeup and counting their money.

"How'd you do?" asked a short blond girl sitting next to Candace.

"Five hundred and seven dollars," lied Candace. It was actually a lot more but she always kept the amount lower when one of the other girls asked. "How about you?"

"Four and a quarter, I sure wish I had your looks."

"Minus two hundred to the club," said a brusque sounding woman sitting on the other side of Candace. "I got me six-fitty, so four-fitty net."

"That nets me three hundred twenty five," continued the short blond. "I have a friend who waits tables at a restaurant and he makes about two hundred a night. This is easier work and I'm making more money so I'm happy."

Candace looked at her face in the mirror as she wiped the mascara away from her eyes.

The club was near the port in Long Beach, in a dirty part of town. It was owned by Tang Tang Fernandez, third generation Chinese Filipino gangster. He inherited the club from his father and then got sent to prison for a stupid mistake, punching an off-duty cop at a baseball game.

They gave him two years.

He still ran the club from prison, and he ran other businesses as well. Loan sharking, gambling, prostitution, drugs. There was a lot of money to be made in illegal trades. Why get dirty digging a ditch or pouring concrete, or be in the electric or pluming trades, when you could make ten times as much money by just providing services that the government forbade.

Tang Tang was one of the top gangsters in the city. He was also Candace's ex-husband in her eyes, although he didn't agree with the 'ex' part. She made a mistake when she was just eighteen years old. Sweet and innocent, and with an incredible face and body, as sometimes happens, most boys were afraid to even talk to her, so she inevitably felt neglected, unwanted.

And then Tang Tang came along, ten years her senior and saw this girl walking to school every day. He was a pro and swooped right in with soft talking and gifts, rides in expensive cars. She had no idea who he really was, and didn't find out till nearly a year after they were married.

She was pregnant with a baby girl, and he started acting strangely, drinking heavy at times, becoming violent. Then the truth came out. He ran a criminal enterprise. Surprise. And then the ultimate surprise. If she tried to leave him, she'd be dead within the week. And now she was stuck. And afraid.

When he went to prison for assault, she thought she could get away, and filed for divorce which would have been approved if she would have followed through. But from behind bars he reached out, with soft chilling words delivered from one of his 'assistants' asking if she loved her baby daughter Belina. Their daughter.

The first year went by and Tang Tang had another half year added to his sentence for assaulting a guard. Still he ran his criminal enterprise from behind bars, with intimidation and fear.

When Belina was two years old Candace made a getaway plan. She bought two bus tickets to Mexico City and applied for a passport. She'd disappear in the country.

Tang Tang found out and was furious. He made his move and had an assistant take Belina away to a safe house somewhere in the city with one of his aunties, or so he said. She would take care of Belina until Tang Tang got out of prison.

If Candace didn't obey orders she'd never see her again.

She hated stripping for money, and yet was forced to do it. The other girls paid the club two hundred per shift to dance, but Candace had to pay three.

By the time she got home it was nearly five AM. She usually took her time in the shower, as hot as she could stand it, soaping from head to toe, cleaning off the body oils and remnants of the night, flashes, memories of strange people watching her.

In the end, no shower would be enough. She could clean the outside of her body, that which could be seen, but for the unseen, the spirit, she needed divine grace, she needed to go to Mass at the nearby church to wash her soul clean again, so she could look at herself in the mirror. To retrieve the spirit that she hid when she walked into the back door of the pit.

Seven AM every day.

And now as though a miracle, not only could she bathe in the fountain of heavenly forgiveness and mercy, seemingly out of nowhere a gentleman had appeared to share the bread of salvation with her. As though part of her prayers had been answered.

She tried to put the thought out of her mind, but she was nearly as motivated to see the young man as she was to plead for mercy and forgiveness.

She got there early, it was twenty minutes to seven and the old woman standing in front of the microphone at the pulpit was halfway through saying the Hail Mary in preparation for the start of mass, and the entrance of the Priest.

She heard the whispers and saw the glances. A sense of pity and remorse hung in the air. Heavier than the normal humbleness that pervaded this place of worship in a Catholic church. The seat next to her was empty which seemed strange. The young man named Fred had been sitting next to her for the past few weeks, had become commonplace, comfortable. His seat was the only empty one in the church this morning, and for some reason no-one wanted to take it. People stood on the sides, lining the walls.

When mass ended and everyone filed out of the church saying their goodbyes to the Priest and attendants, an old woman passed her and said her condolences, stopping her while reaching out to gently touch her hand.

"I'm so sorry," she said.

"For what?" asked Candace. A sense of dread spread from her lungs down through her legs.

Something was wrong and she felt the premonition. She suddenly felt light headed and had trouble standing.

"For your friend who you have sat with all these days."

"What of him?" Her voice hollow and weak.

Other parishioners passed by with furtive glances, making the sign of the cross as they went around the pair knowing that the duty was being fulfilled.

"He was killed yesterday morning, right there."

Candace followed the direction that the old crooked finger pointed towards the parking lot.

The long night of work. The lingering years of worry. The hope for normalcy pulled out from under her, blood drained from her face and all went black as she collapsed in a heap at the feet of the old woman.

11.

The man with his body covered in tattoos sat in the prison cell in front of the computer screen reading, studying every word laid out in front of him.

It was fascinating. Even though the giant prison around him was filled with little noises that mixed and bundled together into one constant hum, he was glued to the screen.

The title of the book was *The Will to Power* by Friedrich Nietzsche. He was intrigued by the essential ingredient; that every being strives to become master over all the space around it, and to push back against all who resist it. And when that being encounters others with a similar aim, they join forces, and conspire with doubled strength for ultimate power.

He was interrupted by a loud voice a few feet away that overcame the steady buzz of the cellblock.

"Tang Tang, you have mail."

The guard pushing the metal cart stood in front of the grey bars enclosing the inmate and held out a wad of letters bound with a large rubber band. The guard's nameplate said simply Cordell.

The man sitting at the table within the cell looked up from the computer keyboard he was typing on and slowly got to his feet. It was a chilly morning on cellblock nine, second floor of the federal penitentiary at Lompoc on the west coast of California, five miles from the coast, a steady on-shore breeze bringing a hint of salt to the air, and even though it was a chilly morning, he was bare from the waste up, tattoos from belly button to Adam's apple, and all down his arms. Even the individual knuckles on his right hand were tattooed, in capital letters CANDY.

"Thanks," said the inmate as he grabbed the wad of letters, then sat back down. He had the cell all to himself, courtesy of a special arrangement with the government that came about in part from a mental evaluation when he entered the prison to do his time, and also due his propensity to committing violent acts, which brought him to this prison in the first place.

Convicted of assault on an off-duty police officer at a Dodger game, he was originally sentenced to a year which seemed like a slap on the wrist to the family of the officer that got the beat down, but it was his first official conviction and the judge decided to show leniency.

During his psychological evaluation Tang Tang revealed to the doctor that he would sometimes wake up in the middle of the night and smash things around him. Lamps, windows, people. Bad dreams drove him to violence without any true fault of his own. He couldn't help himself. Often times he couldn't even remember doing anything wrong and would wake up to a destroyed bedroom without knowing what happened.

The doctor however, did not believe the farfetched story, he worked in a prison after all, and was used to liars and con-artists, murderers and thieves, and they put Tang Tang in a double prisoner cell, but then on the very first night at around three in the morning, screams and thumps from the double cell as Tang Tang and his cellmate were locked in a struggle to the death.

Tang Tang was victorious, pinning his unconscious cellmate's head to the metal bars, the guards had to beat him with batons and taser him before he would let go, and the melee gained him his single cell along with an additional half year in prison for another conviction of assault.

He unwrapped the rubber band and spread the mail on the little table. Every envelope had been opened and the contents searched. The rule was you could receive mail, but forbidden items were nudity, pornography, and martial arts instructions.

One of the letters however was still sealed. An unmarked plain envelope that was stuffed in the middle of the other letters. He had an deal with the guard that delivered the letters. It was simple. A thousand dollars a month to bring a single letter in from the outside, and deliver one to the outside.

While off-duty and in civilian clothes, the guard would visit a coffee shop in Solvang, thirty five miles southeast of the prison. It was a busy place, and there were booths for quiet so people could work on their laptops while drinking coffee and use the Wi-Fi. A waitress would deliver his coffee and a single envelope. He would swap it with an envelope that he had picked up from Tang Tang the day before. Once every four weeks the waitress would leave two envelopes on the table. One was a letter to Tang Tang and the other one was filled with ten Ben Franklins.

The guard was initially hesitant to get involved, but somehow he and Tang Tang seemed to get along. They were both Chinese Filipino, and their grandmothers came from the same province in the Philippines, in the central Visayas, on an island called Cebu.

They figured that they might in fact be cousins. Both their Grandmother's maiden names were Espinoza, and when Cordell looked up the data on-line found that there were less than two thousand people in Cebu City with that name.

"I'll tell you what," said Tang Tang. "The letters are only pictures of my wife. I need them to get through the long loneliness of my sentence. You can open the first one if you wish, in fact you can open any of them to make sure that what I'm telling you is true. Then you'll understand."

At that, the guard agreed. At the coffee shop table he opened the first letter, and that one only. Inside were two sheets of paper with seven pictures evenly spaced. Not just a woman, but a viciously beautiful naked woman writhing on a stage in varying poses. Under each photo was a date, the five pictures from five consecutive dates from the previous week.

"That's your wife?" asked the guard when he delivered the first letter.

"Pretty hot, wouldn't you agree? She dances at a club called Dreamers. It's down near the Long Beach harbor if you're ever in that part of town. You can find her there five nights a week. Go take a peek in person once in a while, if you don't mind and let me know how she's doing."

The guard was tough, but felt the hot blood rush into the pores of his cheeks and he turned away.

Last week the letter that he brought to Tang Tang had more of the same pictures. Five nights with his wife spread out on the stage in the previous week, but this time there were two additional pages. Photos taken at the church seven mornings in a row. His wife sitting next to a man, clean shaven and sitting upright, then outside the church talking with him. A close up of her face. A calm beatitude enveloped her, as though she were a living angel. Happy and content.

Pictures of his wife stripping for strangers in the middle of the night like a wild beast made him calm, there was no danger. Every night he felt as though he were with her, writhing on the floor in unison. They were both in separate prisons and somehow joined together as one.

But this.

Enraged him.

This was too natural, too pure. A young handsome clean cut man sitting with her in church. Day after day.

Nothing in his mind could be worse. He wanted to scream and tear everything in his cell to shreds but remained calm. Revenge would be an easy thing to accomplish.

The letter he sent back was simple: End the meetings now. Publicly. I want her to know that I ordered it.

Leo would know what to do.

Their technique was simple, as though they were identical twins that could read each other's minds. Leo would point out a problem, and Tang Tang would provide the solution. Usually it was easy and the challenge could be solved just as easy in a prison cell as it could outside in the free world.

Their business was in essence delivery of products and services. They would pick up illegal drugs in one location and deliver them to another. Or they would deliver alcohol to a patron in a bar while that patron watched women dancing. Sometimes the vehicle used to deliver the product or service to the customer was an actual car, and sometimes it was a person. They were in fundamental nature sort of like garage mechanics, wrenchers entrusted with maintaining the vehicles so they could deliver their products. Keep them in good working order. Give them a tune up now and then.

In their business, some vehicle problems needed cash to make it run smooth again, and some needed an ax to the chin. A little bit of money to grease a squeaky wheel of the car, or a pipe bomb to blow the whole thing up.

Leo would find a fast car that no one would miss, execute the suiter in the parking lot of the church, escape capture and then destroy the car so that no one could ever identify it.

It would not be the first time they'd used this technique. And it probably wouldn't be the last.

Tang Tang wished that he could take matters into his own hands and solve the problem.

He clenched his two fists and took in a shallow breath, holding it in an isometric contraction. If he allowed himself, he could go on a rampage, pump himself up in this tiny space, release a burst of lactic acid into his bloodstream and go berserk. But this was not the time.

He had to remain steady, pace himself. Keep his emotions in check. He had ten months and seven days until he was released. Three hundred and five days to be exact. He looked at the digital clock on the wall. Red blinking numbers showing the more precise amount of time left. Seven thousand three hundred nineteen hours and fifty five minutes until he was free. A man needed goals to stay focused, to stay sane. The minute column changed to fifty four while he was watching it, bringing a grim smile to his face.

Getting closer.

12.

"Senorita, por favor."

Words wafting into her ears. Her eyes fluttering open, bright grey light with shadows on the edges. A crowd of people stood tall around her. At first she thought she was in a forest of trees and then it all came rushing back to her, a gasp of air rushed into her lungs torturing them and she was awake, sitting on the asphalt, legs splayed at odd angles, upper body and head propped up on the lap of a large woman. An old man kneeled nearby holding a plastic cup of water, it shimmered with the sunlight glancing through the clear plastic.

"Senorita," he implored again.

She shook her head.

"No, gracias." Then sat straight up, gaining equilibrium. She could feel the coarse gravel on her legs and bottom, her right hand was slightly grazed from her fall from grace. Taking one more breath before attempting to stand up. Hands behind and around her lifted on elbows and under her arms, raising her upright again.

She had no idea how long she was unconscious, but for an old man to be able to bring her a cup of water, it must have been a few minutes at the least. A crowd of dozens surrounded her, and she was embarrassed, brushing her hair back from her eyes and looking for the old woman who just a few moments ago had told her the news. She was standing to the right and stepped forward and took her hand again.

"Lo siento," she said, taking a cue from the old man with the water. Then in English. "I am sorry."

"He is dead? Muerto?"

"Yes. Shot in the back yesterday at almost the exact time as it is now. He was your friend, yes?"

Candace shook her head.

"No."

Then thought better of it.

"Yes, I mean of course he was my friend. But only here at church. By chance we sat together during mass every morning. But I only knew his first name."

That changed things for the crowd, and they began to filter away. In some ways the two of them were mysteries to the parishioners who had been attending morning mass for decades.

The two of them began attended church just a few weeks ago, sitting together every morning, never saying more than a few words between themselves, and going their separate ways after the service. Some thought that perhaps they were secret lovers, and that a bitter rival had done the deed. Little did they know that nothing could be closer to the truth.

Candace reached over, put her arms around the old woman and gave her a gentle hug.

"Thank you for telling me. I'm sorry that I fainted. It was just such a shock. He seemed like such a nice young man." Her voice trailed. "I have to go now."

Without another word she began to walk away. A slight glance as she passed the area that the old woman had pointed to. Was there a smudge mark where he'd been laid out? A faint chalk line where his body was marked. Her glimpse was too quick to determine those details. At this point it didn't matter. She began to walk at a normal pace through the parking lot towards her car at the far end. She knew and could feel eyes watching her. The crowd that had witnessed her fainting, even as it dispersed would be watching her for any movements out of the ordinary. Someone even on the far edges of the area would be particularly interested in her reaction, and would be taking photographs.

Somehow, stupidly, she thought that the church was somehow off-limits to her surveillance. By taking side streets in the dark of the early morning hours, overdressing with bulky clothes, hats and sunglasses that she'd evade notice. Of all places in the world where she might feel a few moments of safety and solitude. And now a young man was dead from her foolishness. She could have sat anywhere else in the church, decline his hospitality. Ignore him for his own sake. But she was careless, and selfish in some ways for that type of attention.

It was Tang Tang.

No doubt about it. Shot in the back, that was his signature move. Most other gangsters and murderers abhorred shooting someone in the back, it was considered cowardly, but not to Tang Tang. He had a twisted way of thinking. He thought that the dishonorable badge was worn by the one who was unfortunate enough to be shot in the back. They were the miserable ones who deserved it. He told her one night that if you allowed yourself to be shot in the back then you were lower than a worm crawling under the ground. And then he tapped on her back with his forefinger while laughing, grotesque teeth filled with gold flashing in the glow from the fireplace.

Finally she reached her car, a little sedan with tinted windows, settled into the seat, locked the doors, reached into the center console and placed the beretta on her lap then let the tears flow for a moment. Then she wiped her eyes and said a line from the rosary.

"As it was in the beginning, is now, and ever shall be, world without end. Amen."

She took a picture out of her purse and looked at it. Two year old Belina. Soon she'd be three. She stopped the tears from appearing again. Blocking them. Now was the time to steady her heart, to physically harden it. Everything that she was doing now, was focused on keeping Belina safe.

Tang Tang would be out of prison in less than a year, and he promised to re-unite them. Belina was also his daughter, and his insurance policy that Candace wouldn't skip out of the country. He had her whisked away in the early morning hours while Candace was asleep, and hid her with one of his associates. An older woman that Candace suspected might even be one of his aunties. They sent her pictures of her every week to show that she was being kept safe.

With every week's set of pictures, a subtle unspoken, unwritten understanding that as long as she toed the line, kept dancing at the club and waited patiently they would all be one happy family again, once daddy got out of prison. Tang Tang thought that Candace was still a helpless girl that he could control.

He was wrong about that.

She had a plan, and was getting closer for lack of a better word, to executing it.

Tang Tang's right hand man, Leo had the answer on where Belina was being held. When the time was right, she would strike him down and get the answer out of him. Wait until *his* guard was down, put a bullet in his spine, hog tie him and get the address.

They kept a close tab on her, all the money that she made from the club was deposited in a joint account held by her and Tang Tang. Money could go into the account, but nothing could be withdrawn without both of their approvals.

Another insurance policy to make sure she couldn't run. They gave her a place to stay, a car to drive, and enough food to eat, but that was it.

She was a prisoner living out in the open.

But she had a secret account. Every night she was able to whistle away a few of the biggest bills, tucked into a private place on her body and deposited in a watertight container under a floorboard in the bathroom. After two years she had over seventy thousand cash, which would be plenty to take care of her and Belina south of the border.

Still, Candace had to be careful. Tang Tang was ruthless, but he was also smart.

The year after they were married, he coerced her into dancing at the club. Said it made him hot to see a room full of men lusting after her. It was a mistake, and it changed her.

"C'mon baby," he whispered with his soothing voice next to her ear night after night until he wore her down. "I love you please."

At first she was shy, and insisted on wearing a mask so that no-one would see her face. After being in the club as a spectator for the past year, in some ways she became immune to the process. The women danced on stage and took off their clothes, the men became entranced and acted silly, overpowered by a simple act.

Secretly she told herself, 'I can do that better, my body is way hotter than theirs.'

Like an addictive drug that you're never supposed to try.

"I'll do it once," she told Tang Tang. "And that's it."

It was easy, and in a way she was built for it.

She was hooked and couldn't get away.

She became a regular and started making buckets of money. She'd never made money on her own before, relying just on what Tang Tang gave her, and this was somehow empowering.

One night Tang Tang pulled her on the side. There was a man in the audience. One of his bodyguards recognized the man even though he was wearing a disguise. He was a big shot in the police department. The club was legal and he wouldn't be there as an undercover cop, he had underlings for that. He was there on personal business. Alone.

From the shadows behind the stage Tang Tang pointed the man out to her.

"Do your best," he said. "Let's see what happens. It'll be like a game."

The man was serious as he watched her dance, not taking his eyes off her for a single moment. When she left the stage he sipped on his drink, called the waitress over and asked who the dancer was and when she was coming out again.

"That's Candy. You like her? She'll be out again in twenty minutes. Like clockwork."

A little after midnight after watching Candace dance three times he left the club and Tang Tang secretly followed him to the parking lot to see what kind of car he was driving and the license plate number.

After that he came every night for a week.

Then Tang Tang upped the ante.

"Get close to him at the end of your dance. Lean down and whisper in his ear. Tell him that you think he's handsome and you need a ride home."

"Why?" The thought made her angry and scared. Dancing at the club was one thing with security at the ready, but leaving with one of the patrons...

"It'll be okay," assured Tang Tang. "He's a cop

right? He's safe. We just need him in our back pocket just in case."

While the cop was in the club, they put a mini camera on the windshield, and attached a tiny microphone on Candace.

"Pretty funny, don't you think?" said Tang Tang.

"What is?" she asked, still a bit perturbed by the whole charade.

"We're doing to them what they do us. It's a reverse sting. You think for a minute that he's supposed to be here at a strip club every night? Or that he's supposed to giving a girl a ride home? He's married. We checked on him. Married with two kids."

"That bastard," said Candace, and then shrugged her shoulders. "Probably half the guys in here have the same story."

"Yeah, it's an old story," said Tang Tang. "And that's why we're in business in the first place. We provide a service. *You* provide a very necessary service. If some of these guys weren't allowed to come in here and blow off some steam, they might go crazy and actually blow something up. He'll probably just say no, and head home as he always does."

But he didn't say no.

"Sure," he said. Candace could see the lust in his eyes. "How soon before you can get out of here?"

And that was that. The trap was set. They had a top cop leaving a strip club with one of the dancers after midnight. And then in the car ride home video and audio of him asking her for favors.

Tang Tang brought her along for the meeting with the cop a few days after the midnight ride.

"I want you to see how this is done," he told her and had her listen in on his phone call.

He called the cop and told him exactly who he was and where he worked.

"I own the dance club called 'Dreamers'."

"So what." The cops voice was dull, lifeless.

"I have something I want to give you."

"What could you possibly have that I'd want," said the cop.

"A video. Some photos. The audio portion is the most interesting. Meet me at the restaurant on Fifth and Vine, two thirty." And then he hung up.

Candace and Tang Tang went to the restaurant an hour early and sat at a corner table and ordered lunch. Tang Tang sat with his back to the wall so no one could sneak up on him. He could see both outside the window towards the parking lot, and the front door entrance. It was a good habit. He had Candace sit right beside him on the corner next to the aisle.

A half hour before their scheduled meeting they saw the cop nosing around outside. Casing the joint, trying to look through the windows. He came in slowly through the front door. There in a back corner table he could clearly see and recognize Candy, the woman he took on a ride a few nights before.

His heart didn't sink, he didn't waver. In a single split second he knew what this was all about. He was an idiot and made a big mistake.

It was a shakedown.

In simpler times he would have walked right up and shot Tang Tang with his service revolver, but these were not simple times. He walked straight in, striding normally, and sat down opposite them.

"You're early," said Tang Tang.

"So are you."

"We wanted to get here a little bit early and have some lunch before our meeting. We heard they have some good food here. You look different. No mustache, short hair. I'm sure you recognize my wife Candy though. Except she looks a little different with her clothes on, wouldn't you say?"

"I didn't know she was your wife."

"That's beside the point."

Tang Tang slid the manila envelope over to the cop.

"It's all right there, everything we have."

"You know the penalty for extortion?"

"Who said anything about that? This is a gift."

"What do you want?"

"Nothing, I don't want a single thing from you."

"You're lying."

Tang Tang leaned forward, his voice lowering a notch.

"I own the strip club called Dreamers in Long Beach, it's public information, you can look it up. We run a legal operation, and obey all the official rules, state, federal, and city, although we do bend some of the rules of polite society from time to time."

"Then you have nothing to worry about."

"You sir, work for the city of Los Angeles police department. Drug enforcement division. That is also public information."

"You seem to be very well informed."

"I think it'd be great," said Tang Tang. "If you and I could have lunch now and then, right here at this restaurant, at this very table. Maybe every two weeks, on a Thursday. We could form a little club, you and I."

"What the hell are you talking about?"

"A friendship. Nothing more, nothing less."

The cop looked at him and drew a deep breath before nodding his head.

"Okay, next Thursday, same time. But I'm warning you..."

Tang Tang waved his finger.

"Tsk, tsk, it's not polite in front of the lady."

The cops eyes narrowed, then he picked up the envelope and left.

"And that's how it's done," said Tang Tang.

"How what's done?" asked Candace.

"That's how you form business alliances, friendships, corporations. Empires. Have you ever read Sun Tzu?"

"No."

"The art of war?"

"Never heard of it."

"It's a book written by a Chinese dude about twenty five hundred years ago. One of my ancestors I believe. There's thirteen chapters in all, and chapter thirteen, lucky thirteen is what transpired just now. Sometimes you have to start at end rather than the beginning, and that's what we've done today. Chapter thirteen, you see, deals with gathering information, enlisting spies."

It was interesting, listening to him talk. It seemed as though he knew a little bit about everything, and everything about some things.

She never saw the cop again at the club with or without his disguise, or even hear about him.

Tang Tang never talked about the lunch, or offered to bring her along again for another one. She asked him one time whether he ever kept up his friendship, the code word that he used for extorting the poor guy, but he said it was none of her business any longer.

He changed.

Part of it was when he got injured in a fight in the club. And part of it was when she got pregnant.

The injury part was easy to understand. Bouncers, no matter how talented are only good to a certain point. They need to identify trouble way before it gets to the breaking point. Not everyone is manageable physically. And the two guys who went on a rampage were definitely in the unmanageable class. They were fired up when they first set foot in the place, and then after a few shots of tequila the wheels came off their bus. They wanted a lap dance, and then didn't like the fact that they couldn't touch anything they wanted. Grabbing at the girls with their rough hands. The two bouncers on duty, tried to throw them out but were quickly out matched. Tang Tang had to jump in and got a bottle to the side of his head for his trouble, and knocked clean out. Leo pistol whipped the two guys into submission, and the bouncers finally dragged them to the curb, and the fight was over.

The doctor said he had a hairline fracture of his skull, there was some swelling, and they had to operate right away to let off the pressure.

It just seemed that Tang Tang was never quite the same after that. Then she got pregnant and he really went off the rails. Said he wasn't ready for kids. She wasn't ready for kids. But she was a Catholic and there was no way in the world that she was going to have an abortion. For the first time being with him she was just a little bit afraid, and that was the hardest thing to understand. He always seemed ready to protect her until that moment in time.

He was in his empire building phase he told her. He started spending less time at the club, and more time with other projects. What they were she had no idea, but they always included Leo and a couple of other shady characters. He never introduced anyone to her. They came and went, day and night.

One time she overheard him telling someone over the phone, no a few times, and then with a tinge of anger in his voice that nothing should ever be delivered to the club. Ever. The club he inherited from his Dad was never to be used for whatever outside projects he was now involved in.

One afternoon they took a drive downtown and he had to pull over to use the bathroom.

"Stay in the car," he said. "And keep the doors

locked."

There's a certain type of smell that money has. Actual physical cash. You can sense it whenever you walk into a bank. Piles of thick pliable paper and ink, and not just any ink, but the indelible kind, a secret mixture of color shifting green, black, and metal that emits a chemical aroma, and not just any type of paper, but a combination of linen and cotton, resin, chloride and glue, that adds a tang to the scent.

That was the smell that she recognized coming from the tote bag on the back seat, and being naturally curious she leaned back and opened the zipper. It was stuffed full with bundles of money, green fist shaped packets held together with rubber bands. Some of the bundles were twenties, but most of them were hundreds. Benjamin Franklin's face, long hair, round eyes and tall forehead packed tight in a bag. She did a quick calculation, there was about fifty bills per bundle, which would make it five grand per bundle, and it looked like there was at least forty to fifty bundles total. Maybe two hundred thousand, or close to a quarter million sitting a bag. She zipped it back up and pretended to be looking at her nails when he came back to the car. Good luck with that.

"Did you look in the bag?" he asked her.

"Why should I?"

"Because you're a woman."

"I smelled something. I thought maybe it was dirty laundry that needed washing."

They never talked about it again. She figured that he did it on purpose, left her in the car alone with the bag of money so she could get a small glimpse of what he was doing in his spare time.

With the baby on the way she stopped dancing, and stopped going to the club. She got big, then giant and he stopped coming home at night. Sometimes he'd come home to take a shower and sleep in the spare bedroom, but for the most part he left her alone and they became strangers.

When she went into labor she had to take a taxi to the hospital. He came the next day after she was born. She named her Belina after her grandmother.

13.

Leo 'the lion' Andrade sat at the car watching the door front door to the apartment building.

Loan shark, hitman, bodyguard, thief. Thickly built, soft spoken and brutal in a fight.

Wade, the old man's nurse still owed him money for a couple of bad bets. Bad bets for Wade that is. The car was partial payment for the interest on the money owed.

Now it was time to collect on the rest.

Something told him that once the car was lifted from the old man's house, Wade would try to take a walk, far far away. Try to walk away from his responsibilities. It was human nature. He hadn't wanted to deliver on the car, but it was either that or a few broken bones. Leo had been in the business long enough to know that Wade was up to no good.

Now he wasn't answering his phone, although by the tracking software, Leo knew that he was at home. The door to the apartment building opened and two men walked out, a medium sized white guy in an overcoat, and a thick set black guy in a leather jacket. They stood on the front step, watching the street before heading down to the sidewalk and walking in the other direction.

Leo had never seen either one of them, had no reason to fear them, and yet for some reason they intrigued him. Their body language, the way they walked. They were either undercover cops or criminals, he couldn't tell which. Both animal species looked the same. They definitely weren't civilians. You could tell by the way people's faces watched the world around them. How they interacted. Precognitive defense mechanisms. These guys had it. Unmistakable.

They walked across the street, got into a dark sedan with tinted windows, pulled away from the curb and drove past the car Leo was sitting in. Instinctively he tilted the seat all the way back, then slid down into the driver's seat until they passed, then raised his head looking into the side mirror at the license plate and made a mental note of the number.

The car turned right at the corner and the street was quiet again. Leo got out, and headed towards Wade's apartment building, walked up the steps and into the lobby, two flights up the stairs and stood in front of his door. It wasn't closed all the way, open a crack with the latch resting against the jamb. He reached into his left pocket, taking out the leather gloves and nestled his fingers into them, pulling them the top edge past his wrist, then bunching his fists to make them tight. Inside the apartment he could hear light cursing, Wade talking to himself. He pushed the door open slowly, and walked down the hallway past the kitchen and the dining room towards the bedroom. The place smelled like an armpit.

Wade was in the bedroom, an open suitcase on the bed, back turned to the door, a single dim light hung from the ceiling covered in dust and cobwebs. He didn't hear, or see the man approach him from the shadow of the hallway.

"Going somewhere?" asked Leo.

"Sonofabitch," wheezed Wade as he stumbled over his own feet stumbling against the dresser drawers, breaking one off its track in the process. Cradling his right hand under his left elbow, his face turned white when he saw the face behind the voice.

"I didn't tell them anything," he blurted, then backed up a step realizing his mistake too soon.

Leo's face hardened.

"Didn't tell who what?"

"I mean I didn't tell anybody anything. Anybody." Wade's voice trailed off.

"You just said that you didn't tell 'them' anything."

Wade tried to laugh nervously to hide the mistake.

"I meant them as in anybody. Them, anybody, everybody, them, it's the same thing."

"You sure when you said the word 'them', that you didn't mean the two guys who just left this place? The white guy and the black guy? They just left the front door of the building not two minutes before I walk in your door."

"Nope, I don't know what you're talking

about Leo. No one was here. Nope, nope, it's just me."

"So let me ask you again Wade, you going somewhere?"

"You mean this? Oh no, no, no. I'm just straightening up the place. Rearranging stuff. Got too many clothes in the drawers so I'm gonna store 'em in the suitcase for a while. Might just give 'em to the salvation army or something."

"What's wrong with your hand, why do you have it tucked under your elbow?"

"Oh, just got a little sprain."

"Little sprain huh?"

Leo lunged forward, reached out his right gloved hand, catching Wade before he could retreat any further and yanked the hand out from under the protective elbow. Wade yelled out in contorted pain, falling onto his back while holding the broken hand in the air holding the wrist for support. The thumb from the tip to the lower part of the hand was black and blue.

"Looks painful," said Leo.

Wade huffed and puffed, waiting for the shocking pain to subside before he could answer.

"Yeah, it is. I think it's broke. I think I better go to the hospital and get an x-ray."

He recognized the merciless look on Leo's face and what it portended. The grey dead eyes. Time to think fast on his feet again.

"I fell on the curb outside. Maybe I can sue the association and get some money out of it."

"That's really why I came here in the first

place," said Leo. "We need the rest of our money."

"I did what you told me," pleaded Wade. "I got you a fast car. You said that would cover me till next week."

"I changed my mind Wade. You see I've been around. I can feel it when someone's putting the fade on me. Playing me for a fool. For a sucker. Lying to me. I figured you might be thinking about skipping town, so that's why I decided to take a ride over here to talk you out of it. And sure enough I find you packing a suitcase which is what I figured might be happening. What I didn't figure on was a couple of guys breaking your knuckles, and you telling them something that you shouldn't have told them."

"I swear Leo, I fell and broke my knuckles all on my own."

"You sure someone didn't help you?"

"I swear it. I swear it..." the last words trailed out from lips. He was suddenly tired. It was over.

"Here's what's going to happen Wade. You're going to tell me everything right now. Who those guys are, and what you told 'em."

Wade started to get a second wind, and was about to continue denying everything when he saw Leo take the gun out from under his armpit. It was square in shape, both handle and barrel, with a round silencer on the end. The skin from his neck up vibrated as the blood drained with fear. It was hard to breath. He hung his head and closed his eyes.

"They knew about the car. They went to the

old man's house and that's when they must have found out that I was the caretaker. And then they tracked me here."

"So you have been lying to me."

"I didn't know what else to do. They said their friend got shot in the back this morning, and they thought I did it. They broke my thumb and put a gun in my face. Said they were going to kill me."

"Did you tell them about me. Wade?"

Wade's face lowered closer to the floor. Sobs began to take over his breathing. Mucus filling his nasal cavities. Tears welling up on the edges of his eyelids. He tried to reach out for Leo's feet to beg for mercy but he backed away. When Wade looked up the gun was aimed at his face.

The question was asked again.

"Did you tell them about me?"

Wade couldn't answer, and just nodded his head, blubbering. "They have your phone number, that's all."

"What's their names."

"They didn't tell me." Then he had a bright idea, and his face lit up. "All you have to do is change your phone number and they can't track you."

He looked hopefully at the face behind the hand and the arm holding the gun.

"Sure, that's all I need to do. Just change my phone number."

Wade's optimistic face slackened at the absurdity of it.

"Turn around and look away from me," said Leo. "I don't ever want to see your face again."

Wade slowly swiveled his frame until he was facing the wall behind him. He felt two muffled thuds like hammer blows on his back, and then everything went from blinding white, to grey, then black.

Leo holstered the gun and looked around the room. Even if there was money hidden somewhere it wasn't worth looking for it now. He'd been careful not to touch anything. Fairly confident that not even so much as a single hair from his head had dropped to the floor.

Wade was a small potato. Homicide wouldn't throw everything they had at this case.

But he made a mistake, thought Leo, telling those two guys about me.

Whoever those guys were, he needed to track them down before they tracked him down. Beat 'em to the punch. They couldn't be cops. He had a license plate number and could access the DMV for the owner. Find out where they live. Get a jump on them.

He turned and headed to the door, double checking to see it there was a security camera inside the apartment. He knew there might be one outside and dipped his head while walking to the car.

The burner phone that he used to call Wade was at the apartment. He'd need to smash it and send it swimming down the sewer pipe. Never use it again.

14.

"Hey Candy, your boyfriend's here," said the short blond woman sitting next to her in the dressing room. From their vantage point they could see Leo coming across the stage, and all five of them quieted down and concentrated on taking off makeup and getting ready to leave. The curtain was drawn and the bar help was closing down the club.

"Nice show," he said. He was a man of few words around the women who worked in the club, both the strippers and the waitresses.

Some of them wondered just which way the wind blew with him, but were afraid to talk about it in case someone overheard them. He was silent and creepy, conveying a sense that the thoughts streaming through his mind might be over the edge. Some of the girls thought it might just be a cover. A tactic to intimidate, maybe a survival strategy that he'd developed to handle the potential for trouble that was always one step away in this line of work. He was all business and that was fine with them, as long as they were safe both on stage and while leaving the club, and made enough money to make it worthwhile, he could be as cold as he wanted.

He wasn't always in the club, sometimes weeks went by without seeing him, but when he did show up they all knew it. The vibe got a little more intense, even the bouncers and the bartenders felt it. Ever since Tang Tang went to prison a sense of uneasiness pervaded everyone who worked there, none of them knew how long the club would stay open. He handed an envelope to Candace and she stuffed it in her purse until she got home.

The bouncers escorted all of the girls to their cars and made sure they left safely.

By the time she got home to her apartment and locked the door behind her it was nearly four thirty in the morning. The first tint of grey was showing over the mountains to the east through the window. She still needed to take a long shower and get to mass. It would have to be a new church. She could never again go back to the one where she and Fred shared the holy bread.

She closed the thick drapes and turned on all the lights. What was needed now was illumination. She pulled out the envelope, opened it and studied her weekly picture of Belina. Her stipend to keep her on a straight track.

Her baby.

It was close-up, her baby's face filling half the center of the photo. She was wearing a pair of large sunglasses, with a goofy smile, sitting on the end of a slide at some community park. In the background she could make out swings, a sand box, and even farther away basketball courts.

This was the photo she'd been waiting for. Her breath caught in her throat, and her pulse raced as she opened a drawer and took out a magnifying glass. Every single picture for the past year had either been inside a house, or in an enclosed back yard with no identifying features.

This was the jackpot.

She studied the photo with the thick round glass, pulling it as far away as possible to get the widest amplification. Sure, there were thousands of parks in California that looked exactly like this one. But whoever took the picture made a mistake. Her baby was wearing big reflective sunglasses, and there in the reflection were three definitive objects. They were distorted out of proportion with the round shape of the glasses, but with a little help from the magnifying glass she could see a hill with a radio tower, a mall with a large clock on a pole, and half of the person taking the photo. The person who had Belina.

It was a woman. A very old woman, aged around seventy five she guessed, with long grey hair cascading over her shoulders. She could see the right edge of her face, and the hand holding the camera. On her wrist was a string of large blue stones. Turquoise.

"You bitch," whispered Candace, then she tried to pull back the curse. The woman after all was caring for her baby. Maybe the woman didn't know what she was doing. Candace looked at the photo for a moment longer, the hill, the mall, the woman with the turquoise. Then she went to the cabinet and pulled out a photo album. The wedding photos.

It was a small event with less than thirty people. Mostly Tang Tang's family, on his side of the isle about twenty five people, and her side four including herself. Two aunts, one uncle and her best friend. Her parents long gone. No one on her side of the isle wanted her to go through with the marriage but in the end they all relented and put on their happy faces for the event.

One photo in particular caught her eye. The group photo with the priest and the altar in the middle, the bride and groom standing together in the foreground, the wedding party spread out behind them.

There she was, on Tang Tang's side of the isle, back right hand side in the flower dress, greying hair, wearing sunglasses was an old woman dangling her arm over the man standing beside her, and on that woman's wrist blue turquoise.

The young man standing beside her was Leo.

Candace could not for the life of her remember the woman's name. Some old fashioned name that wasn't' used very much anymore. She kept turning the pages of the album till she reached the pages from the guest book and ran her finger down the list.

"Verna," she whispered. "Verna Sanchez." Tang Tang's step auntie on his father's side, and

Leo Andrade's grandmother. It was a strange family relationship. She was the woman reflected in Belina's sunglasses. She was the woman who was holding her baby hostage. She could be anywhere.

When they first got married Tang Tang bought Candace a laptop computer and installed a search app. It was for security.

"This is how we find out who the people we're dealing with really are. It has property owned, current addresses, cars, phone numbers, court records. Go ahead and try it out," he told her and she punched in her own name and saw her life spread out in front of her. Then she punched in Tang Tang's and saw the multiple addresses, cars, phone numbers. He had no arrests, not even a parking ticket.

She punched in Verna Sanchez, California. In the result section it showed her age as seventy five years old, no vehicle, no property, and her current address was 401 Calente Avenue, Cerritos, California.

"Cerritos," whispered Candace.

Just twenty miles away. She could be there in half an hour. It was nearly five in the morning on a Monday. She didn't have to be back at the club until nine o'clock that night. It wasn't even a choice or a decision, she wrote down the address, grabbed her keys and bolted out the door.

15.

Soon, thought Tang Tang as he sat in his cell listening to soft music, I'll be out again. And this time I'll be smarter. He learned a lesson. Let your temper get out of control and bad things can happen. Being in prison wasn't the worst thing in the world, being dead would take that prize. No, being locked up wasn't the worst thing in the world but it ranked right up there in second place.

He chanted his mantra.

Never again will I step out of line where they can nab me.

Everything was going smooth before he punched the off-duty cop at the game. The club was running smooth, the gambling section was expanding, but the real money, the big juice was starting to pile cash into their pockets.

When he saw the cop in the club that night he had an idea. Somehow it came to him in an instant, like a flash out of nowhere.

Nicco, his top bouncer was busted a few years back peddling crack on a street corner down in

Huntington Beach, and the guy who nailed him was a young undercover dick wearing a disguise.

The guy had long shaggy black hair, and a bushy black mustache. Nicco thought it was funny at the time. It was ridiculous. Thought the guy was wearing it so no one would recognize him buying drugs. He didn't think it was funny when the guy pulled out a badge and a gun and put the handcuffs on him.

In some ways it was a godsend, Nicco spent a year behind bars, got sober, gained weight, and stopped doing things that could get him sent to prison. But he never forgot the young up-and-coming narc. He followed his progress up the ranks. He sat in on trials where the narc was a witness, he watched as the man got older. He found out where he ate lunch and got his coffee, and parked nearby once in a while just to see who he was hanging with. Some might say he was stalking him, but it was just a game. It was public information. He wasn't going to do anything, he was just keeping tabs on him. Like the paparazzi. So when Nicco saw the narc in the club, wearing a disguise very similar to the one he was wearing when he busted a young Nicco on that street corner more than half a dozen years ago, he nearly fell off his chair.

He called Tang Tang over and told him the story.

"Remember I told you about the narc who nailed me when I was young and stupid?"

"Yeah?"

"Well there he is right up front."

At first Tang Tang got a shiver up the nape of

his neck, but then gritted his teeth. They were legit. Everyone who worked for him in the club knew the rules, bring drugs, buy drugs, or sell drugs in the club and you're out on your ear. Zero tolerance. Do whatever you want outside the establishment but once in the front door keep it clean so they could stay in business. The club was a cash cow and they all needed it to keep rolling in the dough.

"You still following him?"

"Yeah, it's a kind of like a hobby."

"What's he doing here?"

"Beats me. He's married now, has two kids."

"How's his wife look?"

"Cute when they first got together. She's getting a little ragged around the edges lately though, I think the kids are dragging her down."

Tang Tang looked at Nicco quizzically.

"Dang buddy, you really are stalking this guy. What's he been up to lately? Any big hauls?"

"I think so. Last week I heard his department intercepted a big cocaine shipment. A hundred pounds, about two million bucks worth."

Just the sound of the word million caused them both to be silent, mulling over the implications. A million dollars was a lot of juice. But two...

"Maybe his target is one of our patrons," said Tang Tang. "We better be careful not to dragged into anything."

They watched him closely for a while from the shadows near the bar. He sat at a table by the stage sipping his beer. His eyes never wavered from the stage.

The man's focus of attention was clear. He was there for the skin show.

Tang Tang smiled when he realized it.

"Well, I'll be damned," he whispered. "He's human."

And that's when it hit him.

This guy was in on some of the drug biggest busts in the city. He had inside info on criminals who had possession of large quantities of expensive, illegal contraband. That kind of information could be useful. It could make a guy who thought outside the box a lot of money.

Why go to all the trouble of importing the drugs, when you could just take it from the guys who already had it here? The cops were going to take it anyways, and put them in prison. In a way you'd be doing them a favor by keeping them out of jail.

The squeeze was a lot easier than Tang Tang thought it would be. For a tough narc who could bust hard working drug dealers just trying to make a living without so much as an ounce of pity, throwing them behind bars sometimes for life for providing a little substance to a willing client, he sure wilted under the glare of his own injustices.

The envelope with the video, audio, and pictures of him in the club, and then in the car ride making advances towards Candy were enough to make him an unwilling accomplice.

Getting outed as a pervert was his greatest fear.

Sure he tried to get tough at their second meeting at the restaurant, but Tang Tang just smiled.

"Do whatever you want. It makes no difference to me. I'm leading a charmed life. I would just like to ask you for a small favor." He leaned over the table, his voice lowering. "Once a month give me the details on an upcoming drug bust. All I want is a location and we'll handle the rest, we'll get there early and scoop up the goods. No one will know. We'll come up with a code. You can whistle it in birdsong and you'll remain clean as the driven snow."

"Whistle it in birdsong?"

"Figure of speech. All I need is an address. And don't try to get wise and set us up."

The cop was stuck.

"You know, a lot of times we have these guys on twenty four hour surveillance."

"So give us one where you don't."

"Let's get this straight," said the cop. "On the one hand, you have some comprising media of me making an ass out of myself that would mean a sure divorce from my wife, and loss of my job. In addition would make it nearly impossible to find another job in my occupation. On the other hand if I do what you ask, if for some reason I get caught, it would be the same, divorce, loss of job, and also prison."

Tang Tang nodded.

"I'm not an unreasonable man. On the one hand, you're guaranteed to get caught, on other it's a gamble."

"I'm going to have to think about it. If I decide to do as you request, I'll need to figure out if it's even possible. Give me a week. I'll meet you back here on Thursday with my answer."

"Okay."

"And if I'm going to gamble, I'll need some kind of compensation, a split of the proceeds."

"You drive a hard bargain, but I was already ahead of you on that. Ten percent of our take."

The cop shook his head.

"I don't want to take a chance on you getting nothing."

"If we get nothing, you get nothing."

"Tell you what. The first one's free. Then after that every time we meet for lunch you bring me fifty grand cash, large bills in a small envelope."

Tang Tang shrugged his shoulders.

"Okay, give me your answer next week, and I hope it's the right one. I hate to think we wasted all this time."

"I've already thought it over. There's a case we've been working on. I'll give you an address next week and we'll see if you can even pull it off. After that it's fifty grand."

The first hit was the toughest of all. Almost as though the cop was testing them.

It was a stash house in Reseda. The crooks set it up on a month to month rental with a legitimate real estate company. The house was nothing to brag about, a three bedroom three bath ranch style, one floor on a corner lot. The house itself was a little worn down inside and out, so they had trouble renting it for the five thousand a month that the owner required. But it was in a good neighborhood, quiet streets and the rental price was high for that reason.

The front man for the drug smugglers looked

respectable and the background check was clean. He was a business man just looking for a place to call home while deciding whether to stay in Southern California. It could be a three month rental, it could be a year. The requirement was first and last month's rent paid up front, with a thousand dollar security deposit. When the front man gave the real estate agent eleven grand in cash it seemed a little unusual, but the agent shrugged it off and deposited the money in the company's escrow account. And that triggered a blip on the bank's radar.

The smugglers brought over small quantities of cocaine, twenty pounds at a time, and their distributors would drive over and pick it up at the house, then take it back to their clients in the city after stepping on it a few times. It was a quiet efficient operation. There were no parties at the house. No loud cars or obnoxious drunk people. The individuals who came and went did so at normal waking hours with respect. There was never more than three people at the house at any one time.

Tang Tang and Leo cased the house the night before and the day of their robbery. They drove by twice and Leo took pictures from a crack in the window of the back seat. They studied those photos and the satellite photos on-line and came up with a foolproof plan.

They'd go in at three in the morning, cut the power at the box, and bust through the front door with night vision goggles. Unless the smugglers slept with flashlights they could easily be overpowered.

Everything worked perfectly, the house was dark, the guys inside asleep, Leo flipped the main power switch off at the box next to the garage, and Tang Tang used a giant crowbar to wrench the door open and they were in.

The only thing they didn't count on was the giant German Shephard who didn't need light to see. The dog had been trained not to bark, and only to bite, and when it jumped out of the dark hallway and latched onto Tang Tang's leg it was all he could do hold in his scream, muscles and tendons being ripped by a salivating canine with razor sharp teeth. Leo came in behind and put a bullet in the back of the dog's skull, and with that the dog let out a sharp yelp that could be heard throughout the house and down the street.

And then it was on.

Two guys came out of separate parts of the house, one from the back bedroom and one from the front, both with sawed off shotguns. Neither of them had flashlights but the two men at the front door were framed by the outside lights.

Sitting ducks.

Leo was quick and slammed the door shut and all was pitch black inside. The two smugglers fired their shotguns towards the general location of the door, the splatter of the shotgun pellets filling the air in a wide pattern nicking both of the men in their arms and legs.

Tang Tang and Leo with their night goggles and perfect vision calmly targeted the two men and with precise shots brought them down. Leo ran over to both of them and gave them each two shots in the back to finish them off, the silencer on his gun making a thud like sound, like someone hitting a pillow with a wooden ruler.

"Son of a bitch, I'm hit," said Tang Tang.

"Me too. Let's get the hell out of here."

"You search the bedrooms," said Tang Tang. "I'll look through the kitchen."

The briquettes of tightly wrapped coke were stacked neatly in a cupboard next to the oven, like flour ready for baking bread. While a suitcase full of money was under one of the beds.

They'd been in the house a total of five minutes, and it seemed like hours. Adrenaline surging, they walked out limping, Tang Tang carrying the suitcase while Leo carried the coke that they'd piled into a trash bag, slinging it over his shoulder like a hobo heading for the railroad tracks.

They'd parked two doors down, and there were lights on in a couple of the houses that a few moments before had been dark. People who'd been sleeping soundly wondering where the piercing yelp, and the popping sounds might have come from.

Tang Tang drove with the lights off till they rounded the corner of the block and headed north towards the freeway. His leg throbbing from the dog bite and four other places on his extremities that felt like someone was sticking him with a hot poker, he managed a slight smile.

"That was pretty intense, eh Leo?"

Leo however was not a man of many words.

"We're still alive."

They found a middle man to peddle the coke, no questions asked. The price on the street was twenty grand per pound and he'd take it off their hands for fifteen, no questions asked, and re-sell it. Suddenly they had three hundred grand in cash, plus the suitcase that had another fifty grand. Worth it for getting an adrenaline rush and a couple of shotgun pellets. Tang Tang joked that he should get an extra slice of the pie since he got bit by the dog, but Leo said that he took care of the mutt so they were even.

They were in business.

Once a month Tang Tang would meet the cop at the restaurant for lunch with five hundred Benjamins, fifty grand for a tip.

"Well you made some work for the homicide division," said the cop when they met for the second time. "You were stupid."

"How so?"

"You left drops of blood at the crime scene."

"I wasn't there. Don't know what you're talking about."

The cop leaned closer.

"Look, don't bullshit me, and I won't bullshit you. We're in it up to our ears now, so we can either quit right now, make it a one stop shop, or we can try for some more."

"What was I supposed to do, tell them to stop shooting me? Or stop to wipe it up?"

"They've got your DNA now. You're in the database."

Tang Tang mused for a moment. He hadn't disclosed any details of the robbery to the cop. They've got your DNA he said. Singular. As far the cop knew, Tang Tang was working on his own.

"How'd they know it was mine and not those other guys?"

"Little drops of blood all the way down the sidewalk to where you were parked. You get nabbed for any crime and they'll get a sample from you. And that'll be the end of you."

"I'll try to stay out of trouble then."

"I checked you out. You've never been arrested before. Not even a speeding ticket."

"My parents raised me right."

"They ran the DNA through the database, no matches. They don't know whose it is. Yet."

Then he got nosy.

"How many guys were with you?"

"What are you talking about?"

"Don't try to con me, I know there was at least two shooters."

"How do you know that?"

"Two different caliber bullets in the bodies. I got the report from homicide."

Tang Tang shrugged.

"Why do you need to know so many details. Isn't it better if you know nothing at all?"

"Because there's another thing."

"Now what."

"Both the dead guys were shot in the back. What do you think about that?"

"I think they were stupid to be dealing in illegal drugs. It could get you killed."

"Doesn't matter to me one way or another what you do with these guys. Our hands are tied when we nab 'em, most of the time anyways.

Unless they start shooting at us. The funny thing is that the bullets in the back were from a single caliber. So it was one guy doing that."

He said it was a funny thing.

"Another thing, the bullet in the dog's head was from the same guy doing the back shooting. Little things like that tend to intrigue the homicide guys. They were going to just pass this off as a rival gang hit. You see they have a lot on their plate and there's only so much they can do with any particular case."

Tang Tang's leg still throbbed from the dog bite. The damn mutt had it coming.

"I'm giving you these tidbits of information so you can succeed in your new occupation. Here's your next assignment."

He slid a single piece of paper across the table. It wasn't an address, it was a car. On it in typewritten letters the make model color and license plate number.

"This car is coming in from El Paso next week Saturday a little after sunset. It's a small sedan, indistinguishable from about a million other sedans on the highway at any given time. The only difference with this one is that it's coming across the border with fifty pounds of coke in the gas tank. If all goes as planned, it's being delivered to a body shop in La Habra sometime before dawn on Sunday morning. It's an eleven hour drive through the middle of the night, so the driver should be a little worn out by the time they get here. It's a moving target, but should be a little easier than your last hit. We have a team ready to nab them at the body shop after they remove the tank. All you have to do is intercept the shipment before it gets there."

In an instant Tang Tang could see it in his mind. Stop the truck, load it on a trailer and take it to their own body shop.

"One more thing," said the cop. "The price went up."

"What the hell you talking about?"

"This shipment is worth a million bucks. I want a hundred grand for every tip going forward."

"We already have a deal."

"Things change."

"Don't forget about the pictures and the video we have. You wouldn't want your wife to be disappointed. Would you?"

"Like I said, things change. My wife left me and took the kids. Your initial leverage over me is gone. I could care less about that now. Now your only leverage is getting these tips in the first place. Sure I could go to jail. But now I have something for you."

He slid a photo across the table. It was a close-up of Tang Tang and Leo leaving the house with the sack of drugs and the suitcase.

"Keep this as a memento, a little keepsake from your night on the town. I have a lot more. Like an insurance policy. Turns out the house across the street was vacant. The owners on vacation in Florida. It's amazing what you can find out if you want. And it's amazing what a telephoto lens can capture."

"Yeah," said Tang Tang. "Just amazing. Why ask all those questions if you knew the two of us were there."

"I was testing you. Don't forget, I've been a cop for a long time."

A dirty cop, thought Tang Tang, without any remorse or regret. Better dirty than clean in the business they were now in.

"Okay," said Tang Tang. "A hundred grand moving forward. Just don't give us any bogus tips."

16.

The car was easy. They had a five man team set up. Three cars and one tow truck. Five miles outside the city, an hour before dawn, the first car that was parked in the shadows and hidden by a row of bushes, spotted the smuggler's car zipping by. It followed in hot pursuit while radioing ahead to the other two cars that were waiting a mile ahead. Those two cars entered the roadway and fell in line in front of and to the right of the drug runner. They boxed him in, front rear and left side.

Leo, who was sitting in the passenger side of the car on the left rolled down his window and shot out both the front and rear tires, causing the car to steer towards the left and nearly out of control, the two wheels shedding the broken rubber and screaming on bare metal rims. The two cars collided and the one on the left held it's line, metal grinding. The driver struggled with the wheel, and was forced to either slow down or crash. He pulled to the right side of the highway on the shoulder with all three of the other cars still pinning him in place, hoping at this point in time that the police patrol car would see what was happening and save him. He grabbed the handgun, slid across the seat and popped out the passenger side door with the car still rolling, crouching, drawing in a quick breath before running towards the bushes. That breath would be his last. Leo, running from behind shot him twice in the back and he slid head first into the bushes.

The drug car was still in gear with the car in front keeping it from rolling any farther. Leo jumped in the passenger side, slid into the driver's seat, applied the brake and put it in park.

Now they worked quickly.

The three support cars left the scene while Leo stayed with the drug car until the tow truck arrived thirty seconds later. It pulled past the sedan, backed up and the driver leaped out, rolled the straps back and under the front suspension, lifted the front end and jumped back in the truck while Leo put the sedan in neutral and stayed put for the ride to the warehouse garage they had set up less than a mile away.

They put the sedan up on blocks, drained the gas tank, removed it from the frame and accessed the interior from the lid bolted to the top and hidden from inspection. There in the cavity, a hundred tightly packed bundles.

By the time the sun was rising less than an hour later, they had the stash hidden under the seats of the tow truck, heading back to the city.

Three miles away, the drug smugglers support crew waiting in the garage began to get anxious. The shipment was overdue. Being an hour late for an eleven hour run meant that something happened. The only question now was how bad was it, because it couldn't be anything good. How long before they called it and crawled away from the body shop.

The cops in the task force waiting on the edges of the warehouse were also getting antsy. They'd been on edge for over two hours now, weapons ready. Prayers said. Ready to pounce and make a name for themselves, and hopefully not die in a rain bullets for their trouble. Their spotter ten miles out saw the sedan with the drugs go by over half an hour ago and radioed ahead to get ready. Maybe they got the rendezvous point wrong. Maybe he ran out of gas, or changed his mind. Heated words were traded. Two men from the body shop left by the side, looked furtively around then went back inside.

The captain in charge of the task force ordered everyone to stay in place and sent one man in an unmarked car to backtrack the ten mile stretch of road. Twenty minutes later he saw the broken glass, and the metal skid marks on the road where the bare tire rims scarred the asphalt. He pulled over to have a look, got out of the car, and that's when he saw the shoes sticking out, well off the edge of the road under the bushes.

17.

401 Calente Avenue. The address rolled through Candace's mind as she drove. The offramp looped around then under the freeway and over the dry Santa Ana river bed heading north. A passenger jet flew low overhead in front of her, making its final approach to the Long Beach airport. Just like the reflection in Belina's sunglasses.

Ten minutes later she turned onto Calente Avenue, a wide street with overhead power and telephone lines, large lots with a mish mash of homes, mostly single story stucco with tile roofs to withstand the blistering heat that would come with summer. Most of the houses had the address positioned over the porch so it was easy to see. She rolled past 401 keeping her eyes straight ahead, holding her breath, heart ready to leap out of her chest if she saw even a single hair from Belina's head. Rolled past and kept going until she was two blocks away before doing a U-turn and going back. She stopped on the opposite side of the street ten houses down and put the visor down in front of her to shield her face as she studied the house.

She half expected to see Leo crawl out from a rock in front of the house. It would make sense in a way. He was the one who delivered the photos to her. Verna didn't have a car, or so the tracking app said. Plus Leo was a freak, with some sort of sixth sense. It was about four years ago when she asked her new husband about his creepy business partner.

"Don't worry about Leo," said Tang Tang.

"Why's that?" asked Candace.

"You ever heard the term 'eunuch'?"

"No."

"Sumerians? Mesopotamia?"

"Are you making fun of me?"

"It's a place in the middle east just north of the Persian Gulf. The cradle of civilization. That's where it all started. It's probably where the Garden of Eden was located. Where the Tigris and Euphrates rivers merge into a lush delta. Mesopotamia, the word itself means between the rivers. Four thousand years ago it was a tropical paradise."

"What does that have to with Leo?"

"It doesn't really have anything to do with him. I was just making a comparison. You see way back in time, a couple thousand years ago, these kings in Mesopotamia came up with a brilliant idea to protect their women. They had harems full of beautiful wanton babes, laying around on pillows all day, combing their hair, bored. What do you think's going to happen if they have normal men guarding them? Eunuch comes from the Greek, guarding the bed. A eunuch is a man who's been castrated and can't have sex."

She put her hand quickly over her mouth in surprise.

"That is so gross. You mean Leo..."

"Yeah, Leo. It was an accident. He got injured."

"No wonder why he seems so crazy. He can't...." She couldn't complete the sentence, but she still had basic bodily function questions. "How does he? Never mind." She shook her head in disgust at the thought. "But wait a minute. Wouldn't that make him less aggressive, like what happens with animals? I remember my uncle raised pit bulls and he said the ones that were fixed were less likely to attack."

"Sometimes I think he overcompensates. The eunuchs back in old Mesopotamia were feared by the kings enemies. They were loyal and trusted and fierce combatants. And I think there's a reason for that after getting to know Leo over the past couple of years. You see he doesn't have anything else to do. Protecting the business, exerting his will over any enemy that that tries to muscle in on us. Those are the moments he lives for. In essence he gets off on violence."

"He's creepy."

"But safe. We're never going to have to worry about him, I can tell you that with confidence. If I ever have a problem, he'll take care of it. I don't even have to tell him what to do which is the best part."

After that things got worse.

One night at the club they closed late. There was a private party and the guests had a lot of cash and wanted to keep the festivities going well past three in the morning. They made more money that night than they usually made for an entire week. The groom was the son of a wealthy hedge fund manager, with a best man who wanted it done right and a few dozen ushers, groomsmen and hangers on. The girls did over a hundred lap dances and if they weren't in top shape would be hurting in the morning. It was around four in the morning. All the booze was locked in the cabinets, the cash was counted and they were headed for the door when the two men came in through a window. They heard the cracking of glass then the distinct tinkle of shards falling on the floor. Two thin gang bangers wearing black masks, each with a silver pistol waving them in the air and ordering everyone to get on the ground. Tang Tang just looked at the two men with pity, while Candace and the remaining girls scrambled to the ground terrified.

It was like Leo fell out of the sky with a baseball bat gripped tightly in his hands, breaking the wrist of the first guy with a downward swing, then up across the jaw of the second guy knocking him clean out.

Candace remembered the sound as though it was yesterday. As though they were at a major league baseball game and the batter, Leo just hit a fastball over the wall for home run, the crack of the bat against the hard ball filling the club.

The first guy with the broken right hand tried to pick up the silver gun with his left and Leo kicked his legs out from under him sending him sprawling on the floor, then took out his own gun from under his armpit, and shot the robber twice in the back. Then he kicked the gun out of the second guy's hand, slapped him till he regained consciousness, flipped him on his stomach and gave that guy two in the back.

The whole scramble of bat cracking and Leo's gun finishing them off seemed to take less than half a minute. It was over so fast that the girls never had time to get scared, then it hit them all at once. Tears flowing, sobs, the works. Tang Tang hustled them all out the front door and to their cars, advising them the whole way.

"Remember, you didn't see anything. You got off work and you went home. And if you do remember anything at all, just think of it as a bad dream. It never actually happened."

He made sure all five of the other girls were okay to drive and watched them pull out of the parking lot. Then he escorted Candace to her car, wiped the tears away from her eyes and looked steadily into them. She could see the anger and revenge burning out through the glazed blood shot pupils.

"Remember, you didn't see anything."

"What are you going to do with them?"

"Burying is too good for 'em. Probably take them down to the pier and throw them in for the sharks and crabs to take care of."

Then he thought better of what he'd just told

her.

"Actually, never mind what we're gonna do with 'em. One thing's for sure, and if anyone on the outside was working with them will know after tonight. This is one place you don't want to mess with."

"Leo shot them in the back," she whispered.

Tears started to well in her eyes again and she squeezed her eyes tight, trying to shut out the memory.

"Yeah, you noticed that huh? That's what we do with rats who try to take from us. They get it in the back. Now forget about it. Didn't happen."

It seemed as though that was the beginning of the end. It was a few weeks after the attempted robbery that Tang Tang got hit in the side of the head with a bottle and had to have surgery to relieve the pressure on his skull. He went from a type of upbeat business savvy aggressive, to sullen angry aggressive. Like a switch went off in his head, and everything turned dark inside.

Belina was her sanctuary, and he let them alone, doing his own thing, staying at the club all afternoon and night every single day. She didn't really know what he was up to, and didn't really care. As far as she was concerned it would have been better for everyone if the bottle to the head put him to sleep forever. She shuddered at the thought and tried to take it back. After all he did give her sweet Belina. They melded together as mother and daughter usually do, coming from the same gentle cloth of humanity. Belina learned how to walk and talk and play, comb her hair and color under the watchful eye of Candace.

And then Tang Tang got in trouble. Gave the off-duty cop a beating at a baseball game and got sent to prison for a year. The day he went in, handcuffed, shackled, telling her not to worry he'd be out soon, she went to an attorney and filed for divorce.

There was a six month waiting period which would give her plenty of time to get out from under his thumb, and get out of the country. She considered doing it a different way and just flee the country with Belina without waiting for the divorce to be finalized, but her attorney recommended against that. Taking a child out of its house could mean the court would have reason to award custody to her husband. So she stayed put. And that was the biggest mistake she made in her life.

It was about five days after she'd filed for divorce. Tang Tang received the divorce papers on the morning of his fourth day in prison. Candace got confirmation from her attorney.

"Whatever you do," she was warned. "Don't speak to him. He'll try to call you, talk you out of it. Coerce you. He may try to threaten you. The best thing to do at this point in time, since you've made your decision, is to let it ride out to its conclusion."

Tang Tang got the divorce papers on the fourth day of his incarceration at eight o'clock in the morning. On the fifth day at eight o'clock in the morning, Candace went into Belina's room to wake her up for breakfast and found the picture on the bed. Belina in her car seat, going for a ride somewhere. There was also a handwritten note from Tang Tang;

'Three hundred sixty days till I get out of prison and we can be one happy family again. I'll send you a picture of Belina every week. You'll be working at the club again till I get back. You start tonight. Don't be late."

The room spun out of control and the carpet rushed up sideways to smack her in the cheek.

After a few shattered moments she regained consciousness and sat up with the note crumpled in her hand and the picture still sitting on the bed where Belina should be.

And that was that. She called her attorney and told her to cancel the divorce. She changed her mind.

"Are you being pressured?" the attorney asked. "If so we can get you settled somewhere else while this process is completed.

"I just changed my mind," said Candace blankly. "A girl can change her mind if she wants to, can't she?"

401 Calente Avenue was quiet. Candace sat in her car tucked and hidden between two big trucks under the shade of a tree, reminiscing about the past. Four years since she was a teenager and decided to get married. A lot can happen in that small amount of time. She went from chewing bubble gum while walking to school in the bright and wonderful outside light of day, to entertaining alcohol soaked bums inside a dim lit club through the late hours after midnight in a little over a thousand days.

Her reminiscing ended quickly as a large silver SUV with tinted windows passed by and pulled into the driveway. A little old lady, thin and frail, gray hair wearing a colorful silk dress with a knitted shawl across her shoulders got out of the driver's side, then opened the back door revealing a car seat with a child who didn't want to be helped out, she wanted to do it all by herself and pushed the old lady's hand away and climbed down onto the driveway and scampered to the front door, long black hair streaming behind her as she ran.

Belina.

Her baby.

Candace reached into her purse and felt the hard metal surface of the pistol and pulled it out.

Square nosed, square barreled, square handle that fit right into the palm of her hand with a round trigger that she curled her forefinger around.

She'd never even seen a gun in real life before she met Tang Tang, but after going out with him for a few weeks he made sure she felt comfortable around them. First he let her hold the pistols and rifles at his house, feel their weight and balance. Taught her safety tips and history, then brought her to the gun range where they practiced for hours with both long and short barreled firearms until she was a pretty good shot.

Now all that training was going to come in handy once she got a clear line of fire at the old lady kidnapper bitch.

She double checked the clip to make sure it

was full, clicked the safety to off, slid it back in her purse and got ready to get out of the car.

Another SUV passed, this one jet black also with dark tinted windows, and she instinctively slumped down in the seat as it pulled into the driveway next to the silver one.

Out stepped a medium sized burly man with a bald head, thick forearms, wearing mirrored aviator sunglasses. He looked around the neighborhood like a fox looking for prey. The lump on the side of his pocket wasn't for a cell phone, it was for a square shaped pistol.

Leo.

Plans changed. Candace slumped farther down into the seat until her head was below the steering wheel, her eyes peering out beneath the top of the circle.

Things had changed, it was now too dangerous. No matter how good of a shot she was, that was in an air conditioned controlled environment. Against the old lady she was guaranteed, but against Leo? No chance.

When Leo went into the house, Candace started the car and slowly made a U-turn in the middle of the street and rolled away. The hardest part was over, she'd found Belina. Now she'd have to come back another day, when she knew Leo wasn't going to show up unannounced.

Soon, very soon.

18.

Poet watched the street as Simon scrolled through the pages on the laptop sitting on his knees.

"Anything yet?" he asked.

Simon nodded.

"Yeah and it isn't very pretty. Leo Andrade, forty three years old, five foot ten, two hundred twenty five pounds. Bald head, black eyes, a scar across his left cheek. He's been arrested seventeen times, the first one, get this, when he was fifteen years old. Five convictions for assault, terroristic threatening, carrying a loaded firearm without a permit, that was his last one two years ago. No current address."

"Jail time?"

"Not much. Looks like a couple of months per conviction along with time served and monetary penalties. They must have thought he was reformed. His last conviction for the loaded firearm he got time served, which was a week in jail, and parole for a year which he completed without event."

"That's it?"

"No. Unfortunately that's not it. He's got a warrant out for his arrest, questioning in a murder case, and the warrants over a year old. They can't find the guy."

"Look up the case number."

"Way ahead of you pal."

Simon typed into the keypad, scrolling through pages.

"Case number 23175. July the 7th, 2019. Two ex-cons, Gordon Phillips and Hermano Sanchez along with a German Shephard dog, gunned down at a private residence in Reseda at three thirty in the morning. Witnesses heard popping sounds and a dog yelping. Two men were spotted leaving the crime scene in a non-descript car. Cocaine residue was found in the house, scales for weighing, plastic bags for sealing. The dog was shot in the back of the head, and the two men..."

"In the back," finished Poet.

Simon looked over at him.

"Yeah, each man with two shots in the back."

He went back to reading the report.

"Forensics found blood traces at the scene matched the two deceased, and another sample from a couple splatters of blood leaving the scene that did not match the two deceased was run through DNA diagnostics."

"And the winner was our boy Leo," said Poet.

"Sounds like he's got a habit of shooting people in the back, if he's the guy who did it. Could have been the other guy for all we know. They got his blood marker placing him at the scene of the crime. No weapons or fingerprints were recovered."

"What about ballistics?"

Simon went back to the report and scrolled down.

"Looks like there were two different guns. One of the deceased had a .38 lodged in his forehead. The other guy had a .45 that entered his cheek and exited the back of his skull. Meanwhile, both guys each had two bullets that entered their backs and exited their chests and lodged in the floorboards. Autopsy says the bullets in the heads were the lethal shots. Forensics says they were face down on the ground when they got it in the back. Probably after they were already dead. Same caliber and barrel markings for the back shots. Same gun for both victims. The dog also had the same .45 bullet enter the top of its skull and exit the chin."

"When was the warrant issued?" asked Poet. He was trying to digest the information. "How quick did they try to get their hands on him?"

Simon paused as he read the date.

"August fourth."

"The crime was committed on July seventh and they figure out some of the blood at the scene matches Leo the first week of August. Took them nearly a month to get it straightened out."

Simon shrugged.

"Maybe they had other, better things to do. Maybe they weren't trying very hard. A couple of ex-con drug dealers, who cares, right?"

"Well, from my experience," said Poet, "it

takes anywhere from a couple of days to a couple of weeks to get the DNA test results from the lab. Then you have to match it against the database which is basically punching the code into a software program and hitting a little button. That part takes five seconds. Maybe it took them more than a couple of weeks to get the DNA from the lab, and they weren't slacking. That's just how long it took. What bothers me is that they matched this guy up with a crime scene where two guys were shot in the back, they issued a bench warrant and here we are a year later and they haven't been able to put their hands on him."

"What are you thinking?"

"What I'm thinking is that a lot can happen in the month from the crime to the DNA match so they wouldn't be able to find him. Maybe he skipped out of the country, maybe he got hit by a train without an ID and got sent to the morgue as a John Doe. Maybe he realized he lost some blood at the crime scene and skipped town for a while. Maybe he just disappeared, went underground and has been lurking around here the whole time. It's a big city. How many people live in L.A. county?"

"Ten million."

"Yeah, that's a big enough crowd to get lost in. The problem is that he's here and doing the same thing."

"Maybe he got tipped off."

"By who?"

"Who else. The dirty cop in the division that Finke is trying to catch by dangling us on a line."

"Maybe we find Leo, and we wrap this up like a little present with ribbons and a bow, and put it on Finke's desk."

"Yeah he seems like a jolly sort who'd enjoy that. Let's go back to see Wade again. He's our one connection that's actually seen Leo lately."

"You think that guy is going to stick around? After ratting Leo out? My bet is he's long gone. We had our chance."

"Let's check his profile again. Maybe there's something we missed. An alternate address, an alias."

Simon punched the name into the database.

"Wade Carmichael. Five foot six, a hundred fifty pounds, brown hair, brown eyes. Thirty four years old. Born January 8, 1973, died January 1, 2021."

"Died? That was yesterday."

"Yeah, remember when I said he was long gone? Imagine that. Guess I was right."

"I wonder what happened," deadpanned Poet.

"No you don't. We know what happened."

"Can you log into the morgue analysis?"

"The forensic report."

Simon pulled up the detective database and located the investigative reports from the day before. There was a lot of crime in the city. Three hundred and fifty reports. Thefts, assaults, robberies. Two murders. He pulled up the first one and there he was. Wade Carmichael deceased. Two bullets in the back. The report says that security footage from the front door of the building showed numerous people entering and leaving both before and after the estimated time of death.

"What do you want to bet that we're on that film?"

"I want to know if Leo is on it."

"It's not on the report yet. Just forensics, bullet caliber, angle of penetration, a general description of the crime scene and the dead guy."

"No photos?"

"None yet."

"Damn lazy cops."

"We need to find this guy."

"Cell phone's dead he could be anywhere."

"I've got an idea," said Simon. "We do a phone record data search."

"What?"

"We have the records of the numbers that his dead phone called right? We take those numbers, put them in a little box so to speak, shake it up, pour them out and see which ones match a different outside number that called them?"

"You lost me."

"If two or more of the numbers that the dead phone called were also called by another different number, there's a likelihood that number was also controlled by Leo, get it?"

"Show me."

Simon took the list of numbers called by the dead phone, copy pasted into a spreadsheet, pulled up a command prompt match and pressed enter. A little circle rotated on the bottom of the screen while the software sorted and sifted like the little box, then three of the numbers were highlighted, and another data field appeared with a phone number in bold.

"Bingo," said Simon. "Let's punch this into the Stingray and see what we get."

He tilted the laptop screen so Poet could see the little red dot.

"Check it out, this system pinpoints the phone to a couple of square inches. It even shows us a schematic of the building where its located. See this? Third floor on the front right side. It's in the living room on the coffee table next to the channel changer."

Poet looked sideways at his partner, narrowing his eyes, holding in his anger, silently counting to ten.

Simon smiled slightly.

"Sorry, I made up that last part. But the schematic does show that it's in the living room, in that building, right there."

They both pulled out their binoculars and focused on the apartment. There was a faint light in the window that was cracked slightly open on the side, heavy drapes covering the opening. They couldn't see any shapes or shadows of people within the room.

Poet looked at his watch marking the time. He was impatient and wanted to smash something or someone.

"Now we wait," said Simon.

"Let's go in there and grab this guy."

"We have him pinned. If he makes a phone call we can tap it and see who else is involved."

"What if leaves the phone where it's at and

takes a jog somewhere and we never find him," said Poet. "What if he's not even in that apartment and we're wasting time sitting out here."

Simon tapped his index finger on his own forehead in the universal signal to use your brain.

"Sometimes you just need to slow down."

19.

They sat in Poet's sedan, sipping coffee while watching the street around them.

Each of them had a pair of tiny binoculars, small enough to fit in the palm of their hand that could switch to night vision. The streets were nearly empty, and it was shaping up to be a long wait. It was like sailing on a boat. With no activity around you and only bland seas surrounding you, the human mind was lulled to sleep. You needed some of kind impetus to stay sharp. Stake-outs were an acquired ability in many ways. You learned how to stay alert. Conversation, if done correctly, made you think, made your mind spin, kept you alert, and staying alert could keep you alive.

Simon took the direct route and asked the point blank question.

"So how'd you end up being a cop anyways?"

Poet took a sip of coffee, clearing his mind before he answered. He had to think for a moment, and that was a good thing. How did he get stuck in this godforsaken pit of a job anyways? It was complicated.

"My dad was always wrapped up in old books. In a lot of ways living in the past. Analyzing, deducing subtle meaning out of words that were written hundreds of years ago about things that for the most part happened to fictitious people put in situations that wouldn't happen in the present day. Sure some of the stories were based on true events, and there was always an element of mystery to them, he imparted that wonderment to us about a good whodunit. But it was all in the past man, and I needed the present. What's happening now. I needed something real that I could see and touch and taste. I needed to solve real problems using my own brain, not relive someone else's. I wanted to *live* the challenge, not read about it. Know what I mean?."

Simon focused his glasses on a man walking his dog on the next block. An old man hunched over with grey hair. The dog a mid-sized white and black Husky, which was a great breed to bring with you on a late night stroll through the dark streets in this part of town. Live the challenge, thought Simon. Yeah I know what you mean.

"I was in second grade. Long time ago but I remember it like it happened this morning. A bully on the playground. Big guy, mean tempered, loner. Throwing his weight around, threatening a few of us for a couple of weeks, methodically, quietly, so none of the teachers knew about it. We were all afraid of him, me especially. I was small for my age at the time, and it really got under my skin. I couldn't eat, couldn't sleep, couldn't talk about it. Till one day I saw him bully someone even smaller and weaker than me. It wasn't a snapping kind of moment where I went berserk, it was more like a calming dread knowing that I might die stopping him, but it was better that than seeing him hurt someone else. I grabbed a trash can, pulled it behind him and stuffed him in. It was the easiest thing I'd ever done, just grabbed him from behind by the shoulders, got him off balance and pulled him backwards, he slid right down into the can wedged tight like a jackknife, knees against his face, and he couldn't move an inch to save himself. he got scared and started crying, screeching like a wild trapped animal, the teachers all came running, and then the truth came out."

"You and the trash cans. You didn't light it on fire?"

"No. but the funny thing is that it was after I was stuffed in that trash can by the black teenagers, I knew how it was done. They taught me the method. I was the hero for a couple of days, but at that age there's so much going on that the event faded. No one bothered me for a long time though. I remember thinking that I brought justice and righteousness to the world, and it stuck with me. I got a bachelor's degree in criminology in three years at college, and joined the NYPD."

"What we're dealing with now," said Poet, "is a little different than a bully on the playground."

"Same theory," replied Simon.

"What do you mean?"

"You know those old stories your dad used to teach in college?"

"Yeah?"

"Shakespeare. What made him so good is that he tapped into the human psyche, that over-encompassing mind soul thing that controls an individual's response to his environment. He boiled down humanity in a nut shell and described it in a way with flowing words that made an observer feel it. The circumstances change, but the human psyche remains the same. It's a dirty world out there and sometimes people are able to rise above it, and others fall into the pit."

"Like Claudius."

Simon nodded, appreciation showing on his face.

"Yeah, like the evil bastard Claudius from Hamlet. He poisoned his own brother so he could take the crown, then married Hamlet's mother and plotted to poison Hamlet, but the scheme backfired."

Poet sighed. He also knew the story.

"They all died miserably in the final act. Poisoned swords and poisoned cups. They dropped like flies at the end."

"Bullies have a few things in common. Jealousy, greed, lust for power."

"You might as well name all seven of the deadly sins, but those will do for now."

"In opposition to kindness, charity, and chastity."

Poet looked sideways at him.

"Chastity?"

"Yeah, that's the opposite of lust."

"We're talking lust for power right?"

"It can manifest itself in a few different ways."

"Because I don't consider myself a bully, but I'm not getting on the chastity bandwagon."

"It's terminology. You don't have to apply it to abstinence from sex. Get your mind out of the gutter."

"Because I'm not doing the abstinence thing."

"No one's asking you to."

"Because I have to get my shag on once in a while, know what I mean?"

"Get your shag on?"

"Terminology."

"Sounds like a type of carpet."

"You wouldn't understand."

"Inner city lingo?"

"Naw. It comes from jolly old England. You should know that it works."

"How?"

"How?" said Poet with a scrunched face. Then he saw the look of mirth on Simon's face. "You bastard."

"Getting back to our man Shakespeare."

"How is he 'our' man now?"

"Hear me out for once, man of dreary thoughts. Put aside your bitter views and listen."

Poet looked at Simon while tilting his head. Then he repeated the phrases while counting on his fingers. Ten fingers for the first line. Ten fingers for the second line.

"Did you just pull an unrhymed iambic pentameter on me?"

"You know what it is?"

"Dude, for the last time, my Dad taught Shakespeare at Stanford all day. But that wasn't enough for him, he had to come home and school me on the old dead guy every night at the dinner table. I'm telling you the guy was obsessed. Still is. Ten syllables. Man, try to slip that shit by someone else and get away with it."

Simon nodded, then continued while taking a quick look at the street with his binoculars.

"Latin was considered the elite language back when 'ol Willy wrote his plays. He wanted to bring a sense of respect to the guttural language of a typical everyday man or woman in the country. Jazz it up. Make the common man walking around London town think he was as fine and noble as someone who could speak fluent Latin. Make them think if only for a few moments that they were as good as those bastards who had enough money and time to go to school and learn it. They packed the theatres to hear the plays. Ten syllables per line made him a lot of money."

"A lot of good it's doing him now," said Poet. "You and my dad should hang out together. It'd be a hoot."

"You didn't answer the question,"

"I forgot what it was."

"You didn't become a cop because you got tired of your old man reciting Shakespeare at the dinner table."

Poet was silent for a moment. And that moment stretched to an uncomfortable pause.

"I only had one uncle. He was on my Mom's

side of the family. He was great, always laughing and telling jokes, always there for birthdays and holidays, he took me and my cousins to baseball and football games, taught us how to fish and how to whistle. We built a go-cart. We sailed boats, climbed mountains. He was awesome. But then he was robbed one night down at Fisherman's Wharf in San Francisco. You know how nice and friendly that part of town is? The heavenly smells, the butter rolls and chowder. He loved to eat food and his guard was down. Someone came up behind him, sucker punched him, took his wallet and started running down the street. He got right up and followed the guy, chased him down into a little alley between a couple of restaurants. The guy pulled a knife and stabbed him a few times and he lay there gasping for life. A couple of good Samaritans, tough guys nearby saw what happened and ran into the alley to help, saw my uncle on the ground dying and the robber standing there with a bloody knife. They got the knife away from the guy alright, but had to beat the shit out of him to subdue him. The guy got off scot free, claimed my uncle beat him up and it was self-defense. My uncle was a black man and to the jury that meant he was dangerous. He wouldn't hurt a fly but ended up dying over a stupid wallet. He was probably chasing after the guy because the wallet had some pictures of his kids in it. He didn't care that much about money. He probably would have given the guy the money if he'd just asked for it. I was eighteen years old, two months away from graduating high school.

My dad wanted me to follow in his footsteps and get a college degree, be a teacher. I joined the Army the day I graduated."

"What about the guy with the knife."

"What about him? What color was he? What do you think? He was white."

"And the other two guys, the ones who beat him up."

"One white, one Chicano. But it doesn't matter does it? The black guy doesn't get justice. But that's not why I became a cop which was the original question that you asked so poignantly. I went into the Army to learn everything they could teach me. I learned every weapon system and took every tactical training class they offered. I was military police for three years. Worked for a while as a prison guard. Then when my four years was up, I got out and went to work for the San Francisco Police Department. I've been a civilian cop for two years. My uncle didn't get justice because the guy he chased down that alley shouldn't have even been on the streets in the first place. He fell through the cracks, and if it wasn't my uncle it would have been someone else eventually. Every time I take someone like that off the street, I pay homage to my uncle."

"What about the guy with the knife. He still running around?"

"Naw, he's in Lompoc last I heard. He's not getting out for a long time."

"He didn't hurt anybody else did he?"

"As a matter of fact he tried to. The cops got a tip. Guy had an ounce of coke and a loaded gun in the trunk of his car right down there by the eastern waterfront in San Francisco, the Embarcadero. He was taking a nap in his car around eleven thirty in the morning when they nabbed him. Surprised the hell out of him and he assaulted two of the cops, then tried to escape. Tried to say the drugs and the gun weren't his. He was on parole for assault and this was the tipping point. He got ten years and has eight more years to go."

"This all happened two years ago?"

"Matter of fact."

"Right about the time you got out of the Army?"

"Almost to the day."

"What kind of gun did he have?"

"Smith and Wesson .38 revolver."

"You seem to know a lot about it."

"I'm an interested bystander."

"You know how he came in possession of the coke and the gun?"

"What are you implying?"

"Maybe if it was me I wouldn't have gone to all that trouble. One bullet well aimed and timed would have done the trick. Save us all a lot of trouble."

"I swore an oath to serve and protect. The thought never crossed my mind."

"I'll check back with you in about eight years. Serving and protecting is a broad term. Having that guy behind bars sounds like protecting the community to me. Anyways I'm sorry about your uncle. Sounds like he was a great guy."

20.

"Phones on the move," said Simon. He had the screen illumination turned down to the minimum so it wouldn't light up the interior of the car and them with it. They watched as the red dot went down a staircase on the schematic and out the front of the building.

Simon closed the laptop and placed both it and the Stingray on the floor in front of him in case he needed to start running after or from someone. They both holstered their guns in their armpit slings and got ready.

He walked down the short concrete staircase to the sidewalk and stopped for a moment looking around at the cars parked along the street, a heavy set man with a bald head wearing a black leather jacket and running shoes. Beady eyes set square under thin eyebrows, thick meaty face and pinned back ears. Like a pit bull of a man. It almost seemed as though he looked directly at and through the front windshield of their car, looking directly at them, but both

Simon and Poet were leaned back in their seats both with binoculars at the front of their eyes.

"You think he sees us?" asked Simon.

"I wouldn't mind if he did," said Poet. "Wouldn't mind one bit if he decided to walk over here and have a little chat with us."

But Leo's attention was diverted by the small crowd by the alleyway next to the liquor store. A little scuffle had broken out, shouts of anger, a bottle broke on the asphalt, then two shapes rolled out into the street wrestling over an object.

Billows of white smoke flowed from the dark alleyway as the hidden shapes took in the action, still puffing on their pipes. Like spectators in ancient Rome watching gladiators battle in the arena.

Leo stepped off the curb into the street, unlocked a small black car, took one more look around, then hopped lightly in, a lot lighter and quicker than a man his shape and size should be able to and sped off down the street, past the wrestlers, turning right at the corner.

"He didn't use his turn signal," said Simon. "That's a moving violation."

Poet started the car and pulled away from the curb slowly at first, crawling past the grimy wrestlers so he could get a good look at them, animals in the city, it was two men, or what appeared to be men, they were so filthy and grimy with matted hair and torn clothes that it was hard to tell exactly what they were, locked in mortal combat over something in a backpack. Once he was safely past them he sped to the corner and turned after the black car.

"Oh no, he's getting away," deadpanned Poet.

Simon had the laptop back on his lap, the red dot moving along a map of roads ahead of them.

Poet punched the accelerator lightly and their car hopped ahead, he zigged and zagged around a few cars in front of him until he could spot the black car in the fast lane two blocks away.

"He's already a quarter mile ahead of us," said Simon. "I think he's speeding. I only hope that he doesn't get pulled over before he gets to his destination. And don't you get pulled over either, last thing we need is to explain ourselves to the authorities while the bad guy gets away."

"I'll just move with the flow, just stay with crowd."

"We're heading west," said Poet. "Towards Long Beach. Is that thing going to work with us both moving at the same time."

"It's working." said Simon.

Two mistimed red traffic lights and they were far behind.

"Just stay straight," said Simon. "He's two miles ahead of us. We got him."

"Did you get the license plate number?" asked Poet.

"I took a picture with my binoculars."

"Your binoculars can do that?"

"Of course they can, can't yours?"

Poet thought about looking over at Simon but stopped himself and kept his flaming red eyes focused on the task ahead.

"Of course they can," he whispered shaking his head.

Twenty minutes later the red dot stopped somewhere around two miles ahead of them.

They were on the outskirts of Long Beach on the edge of the rich side of the city but still on the gritty side. Like the beach that was just over the bend, the water clear and calm representing the wealthy neighborhoods, and the high tide where this neighborhood was set, where all the flotsam and debris was scattered, rotting seaweed, discarded bottles and caps, driftwood and dead fish. The high water mark where all the dirt settled. Hardware stores, flooring companies, auto supplies, all closed for the night, and yet the small bars, and the strip clubs still open.

"Right here," said Simon, and they pulled into the parking lot under a neon sign, obnoxious pink and blue, the shape of a woman's ankle with a diamond bracelet around it shimmering boldly in the night next to the asphalt. The sign said in big flowing letters: DREAMERS.

There were around thirty five cars in the lot scattered around the edges with some parked right in front. Even though they were in the high water mark of society, some of the cars parked in front of the establishment obviously came from the other side of town.

Bentleys and Mercedes, Lexus and BMW. And not some beat up and used models, but brand new and shiny, scattered among trash heaps and work trucks.

"It's a strip club," said Poet.

"You don't say," replied Simon. "I can't remember the last time I was in one. Oh yeah, it was last week. It was strictly business."

"New York City?"

"There's a few here and there."

"Probably a few hundred."

"I worked vice. We go where the business is."

"So you know your way around inside one of these joints."

"They're not that complicated as long as you play by their rules and keep your hands to yourself. With the kind of customers they entertain, mix it with provocative naked women and intoxicants, you can get the kind of combustible mixture that needs a couple of well-trained extinguishers. Bouncers that can handle themselves in an MMA ring, because sometimes that's what it turns into. I imagine with this size crowd they have at least three gorillas working. The problem for us is we won't be able to bring any weapons, they'll have a metal detector at the door."

"I see the car parked on the side. Is that the license plate?"

Simon pulled out his binoculars and focused on the back bumper.

"Yeah, that's it. The car's empty, he must be inside. What do you want to do, stay outside armed and ready in case I need backup, or stick together?"

"I think we should stick together," said Poet. "I already lost one partner, I don't want it to happen again."

"I'm more worried about you than me."

"Don't worry about me pal."

"I mean as far as you being married and all.

Being in a place like this might get you in trouble."

"Stop joking around. Let's go inside, find that guy and see what he's up to, who he's with. If he's on his own, we'll wait till he leaves to nab him. If he's with some other people, we'll put them on our naughty list."

Simon nodded. "Okay, have it your way. This is business. We have to remember that. For the girls working in there, it's also just business for them. They might come across like they're in love with you, taking off their clothes just for you, dancing in your face, nearly on top of your lap, they get paid for it, it's what they do for work, so don't fall into some type of emotional trap and think for a moment that they have any real feelings for you. It's their job."

"Sounds like you're trying to pep talk yourself," said Poet.

Simon turned towards him and shook his head. "I am, believe me I am."

"Okay, well just keep your mind on your business, and not on theirs, if you know what I mean."

Simon was silent for a moment, hesitating.

"What's wrong?" asked Poet. He could tell that Simon was disturbed.

"Just about everything. These places...."

"Yeah, what about them."

"It's like going into a war zone."

Poet chuckled.

"A strip club? Like a war zone?"

"Just about the most degrading places on the face of this planet. Some of the women in there are no different than slaves."

Poet drew in a painful breath and shook his head. "Don't you go talking like that. Don't you *dare* compare being a stripper to being a slave. We don't know each other that well."

"You don't like the analogy?."

"Man, you said it yourself that the girls that work in there consider it their *job*. They have free will to come and go as they will. Do you even know what a slave is? Have you even looked at the color of my skin? Do you know the history of my people?"

"I don't give a damn about the color of your skin. But I do care about the history of your people, and that's why *you* need to be careful. You are currently not a slave, your ancestors may have been, and that is exactly why you might need to check yourself."

"Now why in the hell do I need to check myself."

"Because you don't have experience with these types of places. You said it yourself. You've never been in one."

"Man, do you know the types of criminals I've taken off the streets? I've gone into the grimiest hell-holes on earth, drug dens, filled with thieving murdering scumbags."

"It's nothing compared to this," said Simon. "A lot of these girls are vulnerable, manipulated with drugs and the threat of violence, they're young, in a way innocent, for a while anyways, and they're used like a product, a piece of pretty meat on a platter, merchandise sold to the highest bidder. Some of them were brought here against their will, smuggled into the country. Forced to strip down to their naked skin, like animals in the wild. In my opinion it's the worst crime of all, and somehow it's legal." He pointed to the construction project nearby. "I'd like to go hotwire that steamroller and flatten this place."

"This how you prep yourself to go into a war zone?"

"Yeah."

"Simon," said Poet, his voice even and calm. "I understand what you mean now, about these places. But we can only do so much, and our job right now is to find out who gunned down our partner and bring them to justice."

Simon nodded. It was time to get down to business. He pulled out his wallet and looked through one of the folds, pulling out five well-worn twenty dollar bills.

"We're gonna need cash to tip the girls."

"I don't carry cash," said Poet.

"You don't carry cash?"

"Too dangerous."

"You carry a gun."

"Yeah, and if I also carried cash I'd have to shoot the son of a bitch who tried to rob me of it. So if anyone ever gets a jump on me they can see I got nothing but a credit card and they're shit out of luck. They can try to use the card, but that's a sure fire way to get nabbed and most of the dirtbags out there know it."

"That was one heck of an analogy Poet. I had no idea you lived that careful and precise of a life. Tell you what, you can pay for the cover charge and drinks with your credit card and I'll *loan* you forty bucks to tip the girls. We're going in there on business, and we don't want to attract unwanted attention, the kind you get when you don't throw a little bit of money on the dance floor."

He handed two of the twenty dollar bills to Poet and put the other three back in his wallet.

They put their guns and holsters in the center console. Simon put his pepper spray, billy-club, and taser in the glove compartment and they got of the car into the chilly night air. The light wind was blowing from the west bringing the scent of salt water and seaweed in the parking lot. It was a high tide.

Even here in the parking lot a few hundred feet away they could hear the thumping music pounding through the walls, and as they walked towards the front door the sound got louder till it was nearly deafening, and the front door was still closed.

Standing in front of the thick grey metal door was a thick man in a thin white t-shirt, bald head, tattooed arms, blue jeans and steel toed ass-stomping boots. He looked like a prison guard. Simon noted that the shirt he was wearing was the tear away kind so if anyone tried to get a grip in a fight, or pull the shirt over his head, the cloth would rip apart and not be a trap. He probably oiled his ears with lanolin.

Unsmiling he blocked the door and pulled the metal detecting wand the size of a baseball bat from behind his back. The way he was holding it he could use it to find knives and guns, or beat someone to a pulp with it.

"You guys have any weapons?"

"Nope," said Simon as they both shook their heads and lifted their arms like angels so the bouncer could wand them.

"Okay one at a time. You stand over there till I finish with him first."

He pointed at Poet who backed up a few feet and waited. It was smart, thought Simon, better than have two guys crowd you and overpower you while you were busy leaning over with a wand.

Probably a skin head racist, thought Poet as he backed away and waited his turn. He made a mental note on the way the guy held the wand.

The guy was a lefty, which meant if it came down to it, he could feint with his right and come over the top with a sweeping left hook onto the side of his jaw. One punch to throw him off balance, stun him, then finish him off by coming up and inside with a few short ones to the chin.

"Alright, now you."

Simon stepped back and Poet stepped forward, calm, eyes focused on the wall, his peripheral vision wrapping the xenophobe into the edge of his sight.

The bouncer stepped to the side and opened the door unleashing the thumping beat, and flashing lights.

"Twenty dollar cover charge and two drink minimum. And keep your hands to yourself."

When he said the last part, he was looking directly at Poet, who merely nodded.

If it came down to it, he was ready for the guy at the door. Now he needed to focus on the unknown that was inside.

A wall of thumping grinding music flowed through the door accompanied by a different sensation, crisp air-conditioned atmosphere lightly tinged with perfume, alcohol, and something else that was undefinable, some type of primeval scent that went straight through the nostrils bypassing the piriform cortex that identified scents, and going straight to the portion of the temporal lobe in the brain that drove sexual desire, the amygdala.

Simon moved through the door, eyes taking in the whole picture in one glance, then ratcheting through the priorities, like a quarterback on the football field looking at the defensive arrayed against him before the ball was hiked. Who was blitzing, where the trouble was going to come from. How to stay alive.

The room itself was the size of a small ballroom, fifty feet by fifty feet, square. A long bar to the right, round tables and chairs around the perimeter with a raised black dancefloor towards the back of the room with two gold plated poles on either side, one them which was currently wrapped around with a long legged brunette wearing a white thong and nothing else. Wrapped around the pole with one toe on the ground, the inside calf of her other leg deftly wedged high and tight for leverage, one arm and hand grasping the pole for stability while her other arm free to express its inhibitions, gravitated around the pole with the rest of her body following.

Without making eye contact, Simon looked

for any other eyes that were watching him as he walked through the door. The woman at the pole was watching him. So was the bartender, a waitress waiting for drinks and a few of the patrons sitting at the tables. His persona was non-threatening. He'd learned long ago to slacken the muscle features around his neck and eyes to give off a peaceful vibe, put people at ease, make them unwary of what he was capable of. It was a tactic of war and it also worked for an unarmed individual walking into a dark bar in the middle of the night.

There was an open table just inside the doorway to the left, and he started walking towards it. From here they could watch the dance floor and the rest of the room. Poet following a few steps behind. The eyes that had been watching Simon, along with some new eyeballs gravitated to the larger black man.

A pretty waitress in a dress that barely fit her came over and greeted them with a big smile.

"What'll it be gentlemen, I haven't seen you in here before, have I?"

"First time," said Simon with a big matching smile right back at her. "We heard you have a nice show."

"You heard right. Do you want to sit closer up by the dance floor? There's a table right up front?"

"We're fine here for now," said Simon. "Maybe later after we get loosened up."

"It's a twenty dollar cover charge and two drink minimum."

Simon and Poet each put their credit cards on

the table.

"I'll take a draft beer if you have it," said Simon. "Whichever one you recommend.

"Club soda with a lime," said Poet.

She looked surprised for moment.

"I'm driving," he said with a shrug of his shoulders. "I lost the coin flip."

She laughed lightly, ran the two cards through her portable scanner, and headed back to the bar.

"See our guy yet?" asked Poet.

"Nothing."

The girl doing the spinning on the pole reached her finale to match the end of the song, bent down to pick up the money that was scattered all around, and strutted off the stage.

The speakers went silent for a moment and then ever so slowly a flamenco type song filtered into the club, a Spanish flared song with trumpets and classic guitars. Out from the back of the stage a black haired goddess emerged from the shadows, wearing a long sequined black dress that matched the color of her hair, cut down the side of her legs with a plunging neckline.

Simon and Poet's eyes drifted from searching the room for Leo, to latching firmly onto the woman walking slowly out onto the stage.

Everyone in the audience was doing the same thing, even the bartender and waitresses. It was as though the room had been empty and was suddenly filled with life. She commanded attention from the tips of her barefooted toes to the top of her head and especially the vivid sharp eyes flashing with a heated desire, augmented by the gentle yet firm curves that flowed everywhere below those eyes.

"Holy cow," whispered Simon.

"Hey," whispered Poet back to him. "Don't lose it man. Get back to business."

"What, are you dead?"

"No, I'm married. I see the girl, but we have a killer somewhere in here with us, so don't lose focus and get dragged into something that gets us whacked."

"I think it was Aristotle," said Simon. "That said he was somewhat relieved when he got to the age of seventy and the pangs of lust slowly released him from their grip. I'm not there yet, and sometimes... when I see a girl that looks like this..."

She began her dance around the pole, slowly at first, leaning on it every so lightly with a single long fingertip while looking out above the crowd, not at them, not at anyone. Pouting lips. All angles and jutting bumps. Every eye was on her as she unzipped the side of her dress and slowly stepped out of it revealing tan flawless skin, she let it fall to the floor in a heap, then suddenly and viciously kicked the crumpled dress behind her to the curtain, she kept the mask on, flashing wild eyes as she moved with the rhythm of the music posing with a high bare hip on one side then the other lifting her frame, lifting one arm straight to the sky, then the other flexing her torso, every sinew in perfect shape, a light layer of moisture began to glisten on skin shining under bright lights, she seemed oblivious to what she was doing, in a trance, as though her mind and body even though intertwined were in a distant place and time and she was alone in some type of erotic nirvana, thriving, striving for release, shoulders, elbows, hips moving, stretching.

Men crowded around the stage throwing money at her feet, drunkenly hooting and hollering and begging for attention. She ignored them all, her eyes fixed on some distant place, then she sighed deeply and leaned her shoulder against the pole for a moment, exhausted and seemingly content, then stood erect again, all angles and jutting bumps, as though she'd just woken up from a dream, looking down at the men crowding around the stage with vivid sharp eyes, sending them into more of a frenzy.

Simon got up from the table and walked over to the side of the dance floor which was nearly shoulder high and placed the entire wad of money that he had near her feet. It was then that he saw the bronze moon tattoo just above and behind her left ankle. He stared at it for a moment to make sure what he was seeing was real, and when he looked up towards her face she was looking directly down at him. She had a sudden inquisitive look on her face. He looked back down at the tattoo again, and when he looked back up he couldn't hide it in his eyes, it was the tattoo. Their eyes met, and she was somehow intrigued, usually men didn't look at the tattoo on her ankle. She bent down and slowly picked up the wad of money, inches from his face, her eyes searching deep into his for whatever secret was hidden in there.

Time stood still.

Then just as suddenly the moment was over, she backed away blinking, taking a quick breath of air, picked up the rest of the money on the stage and padded away on bare feet, stopping to pick up the dress and went through the curtain without looking back.

The five minute frenzy on the stage took a toll on the audience and the waitresses, and they needed to re-group, re-load on drinks before the next act came on stage that no one thought could top the last one. It was as though a giant balloon was filled with air and then was popped with a little needle, and that was okay in a way, everyone needed time to catch their breath.

Simon, blending in with the crowd that drifted away from the stage walked back over to the table and sat opposite Poet who was brooding, slumped down in his chair, twirling his drink with a little straw.

"What's wrong?" asked Simon.

"Don't look directly," said Poet. "Put your peripheral vision towards the front door and tell me what you see."

Simon looked down at his drink, getting his bearings, then looked slowly up to a point to the right of Poet's jaw till the front door came into view on the edge of his sight.

"There's a guy at the door. A bouncer. He's looking at us while talking into a headset mic."

"That's what I was afraid of."

"Why?"

Simon looked directly at Poet while keeping a

bit of his vision on the door.

"I'm looking at the stage," said Poet. "My vision hasn't changed since your new friend got on stage. Leo walked out of the back and went behind the bar to mix drinks. He's been looking over here at you and me, then he sent over a waitress with some drinks that he fixed. I could tell that he was talking on a headset to some people but I didn't want to look around to find out who."

The waitress came over and set the drinks down in front of them and put the first set on her tray. Neither of the men complained that they weren't done with the first drinks, they just went along for the ride.

"Thank you," said Simon, then after she walked away to Poet. "You think they're trying to poison us?"

"I think they're trying to put us to sleep so we're easy to manage. One thing's for certain though. For some reason 'ol Leo has us pegged."

"You remember when we first met at the precinct, and Finke had us come in and go out the front door?"

"Yeah."

"I thought that was kind of strange. We're working undercover and going in and out the revolving door for anyone to see. There's a building just across from the precinct and anyone could set up a camera and take pictures of anyone coming and going, pass them around to all their friends. You and me by the way stick out like sore thumbs."

"I think that's a little far-fetched" said Poet.

"He pegged us alright, but some other way. The question is, what are we going to do about it?"

"We're sitting ducks in a little barrel with no weapons."

"We could either get up and leave right now, or play along with their little game. Pretend to take some sips of their magic cocktails, then start slurring, and wobbling to the car where they think they can take us."

"I like the second idea," said Simon. "There's something else though."

"What?"

"The girl that was dancing. She had a tattoo. I think it was *the* tattoo."

"What do you mean 'the tattoo'?"

"It was on her ankle."

"Little golden Aztec moon?"

Simon nodded.

"Well I'll be damned." Poet shook his head and sighed while keeping an eye on the bar. "What if it was a coincidence? What if it's a new fad? What if there's a whole bunch of pretty young women with golden moon tattoos on their ankles running around this town?"

"Sure, that's a possibility. There's probably a giant gang of beautiful Latina girls with golden moons on their ankles all over this city. It's just a wild and crazy coincidence that she happens to be working at the club where the guy who shoots people in the back also works."

"We need to talk to that girl."

"Yeah, well we're not going to do it here."

"Then we have to get out of here."

"Maybe we could play our cop card. I have my

badge with me, what about you?"

"Yeah right. A badge without a gun probably wouldn't make these guys think twice. Even a gun with a badge probably wouldn't make a difference."

"I don't think they're going to let us go peacefully."

"Nor should they," said Poet. "I wouldn't if I were in their shoes. In fact, I'd rather they played their hand if that's what they're planning. I say let's get this over with."

"I agree," said Simon.

The music started up again, pumping grinding, thumping bass and drums, while another beauty strutted onto the stage to hoots and hollers. This girl was way different from the last, unashamed, smiling, happy to be on-stage with hungry eyes crawling all over her.

"Bottoms up?" asked Poet.

"Suck 'em up," said Simon.

Both men clinked the glasses together in a toast, then put the rims of the glasses up to their lips without touching skin to drink, the corners of their eyes on the door and the bar, pretending to take healthy gulps, heartedly swallowing air, then put the glasses back down on the table and wiped their mouths with the back of their wrists in satisfaction and turned to watch the new dancer.

A few moments passed then Poet nodded his head towards his chest as though he was falling asleep. Simon's head tilted to the side and he shook himself back awake and reached out to steady himself with palms on the top of the table. He blinked a few times then rubbed his chin a few times then shook his head again then stood wobbly to his feet and steadied himself with the back of the chair. Both men now were on their feet as though they were walking in jello, slowly and methodically heading towards the front door.

The bouncer at the door opened it with a wry smile on his face and without a word closed it behind them and waited outside while they wandered across the lot to their car.

They turned around to look at him and saw that he was talking into the mic.

"How come you had to park so far away?" asked Simon.

"Seemed like a good idea at the time."

"When's the last time you were in a street fight?"

"I don't get into street fights. I'm a cop. I make it strictly one sided. I tell them what to do and they do it, or I stomp their ass into a mud hole?"

"Mud hole huh?"

"Figure of speech."

"What about you? Wait. Don't tell me, last week outside a strip joint."

"How'd you know?"

"Lucky guess."

"Ever shot anyone?"

"No."

"Well let's keep your unblemished record clean."

They heard footsteps, and a loud voice behind shouted out.

"Hey, you two deadbeats!"

They turned, and there were two giant bouncers walking towards them. The bald headed ex-prison guard and the other guy who was behind the bar with Leo.

"You guys walked out without paying your bill!"

Simon turned to Poet.

"I thought you paid the bill?"

"I thought you paid it," said Poet, and they both shrugged and started walking back to the club towards the bouncers. They each gave their walking gait a little extra wobble when they got close enough for a karate chop, both bouncers on cue took a swing at them.

Poet stepped back, the fist passing by his chin by a few inches, the bouncer put everything he had into it, grunted with the effort, thinking that it was a sure thing, and now with no contact was off balance. Poet came in low under the swinging arm, and with one solid straight uppercut came up under the man's chin lifting him off his feet and he flopped backwards, his head cracking on the asphalt.

Simon bobbed to the side letting the other guy's fist glance down the side of his arm then grabbed onto his shoulder using his forward momentum to pull him closer and popped him straight in the nose, breaking it with a sickening thud. The man slumped to his knees and Simon gave him a karate chop to the vagus nerve on side of the neck under the ear, knocking his clean out.

"Let's get the heck out of here," said Simon.

"What about Leo?"

"He can wait. We need to talk to the girl."

"You know they have cameras all over this place."

"Sure, they have still shots of us and that's okay. Let's make them wonder what we're up to. We'll park nearby, watch with our binoculars till she leaves and then follow her home."

There came another shout from the side of the club. Standing there was a short stout man with a gun in his hand pointing it at them.

Leo.

"The best laid plans of mice and men," said Poet. "Maybe Leo can't wait."

"Robert Burns," said Simon. "The Scottish Shakespeare. The real sentence is: the best laid schemes o' mice an' men. Gang aft a-gley."

Leo started walking towards them twenty yards away holding the pistol steady.

"I see a pistol," said Simon.

"Yeah I see it too," said Poet. "Pointing at my head."

"I mean I see a pistol in the waistband of the guy you knocked out at your feet. I'll bet my guy has one too, if I had time to look."

"Count of three we drop to the ground and use these guys like sandbags, I'll grab the gun and get him," said Poet. "One, two..." Then Poet dropped suddenly to the ground. Simon was caught flat footed and seemed suspended in the air as Leo fired a shot. Then Simon hit the ground face first with a thump nearly knocking the wind out of him, behind the big hillbilly that was laying on the ground. Shots were being fired whizzing over their heads, then a sickening thud and Poet yelled out in pain as he got the gun in his hand and returned fire. Simon pulled on the guy in front of him and found the gun on the ground under his beer belly, then also began to squeeze off shots, carefully aiming at Leo who was now zig zagging and running away from them, bullets kicking up asphalt around his feet.

He jumped into a big black SUV and raced away.

Simon was pissed as he lay there with the smoking gun in his hand.

"I thought you said drop on three?"

"Yeah, one two and drop."

"You didn't say three."

"You're not supposed to say three, it's a given. One, two and three *is* the drop. It's silent action, everyone knows that."

"You're supposed to say three," said Simon.

The guy in front of him began to moan and tried to get up. Simon gave him a tap with the butt of the pistol and he laid his head on the asphalt again, out cold. "Bastard tried to kill us. Hey you're bleeding."

"He got lucky, clipped the top of my arm."

"Let's go get him," said Simon and he jumped to his feet and helped Poet up. "I'll drive while you wrap that thing up."

"I'm okay, it's just a flesh wound."

They jogged towards the car, Poet handed the keys to Simon and he fired up the engine and raced of the parking lot in the direction the SUV went.

"Reach in the back and grab the backpack, I

always keep a roll of elastic bandage."

Poet got the bandage roll and wrapped half the roll tight around and around his right forearm, then tore off the end with his teeth and pressed it down, gluing it tight.

Once they were about a mile down the road and safely away from the strip club, Simon pulled over and got out the Stingray.

"No sense in driving willy nilly into the night. Where are you now?"

The screen showed a red dot, but it was behind them. They'd passed him. Simon put the car in drive, made a U-turn and went back the way they'd come. They passed it again, and it was a dark and deserted stretch of road.

He turned off the headlights and pulled off to the side, grabbed his flashlight from the backpack in one hand and his pistol in the other and jumped out of the car ready for action in case Leo was hiding somewhere in the weeds ready to ambush them.

Poet jumped out of the passenger side and crouched by the side out of sight. A car was heading their way, and Simon put the pistol down on his side hidden with his body, while the car passed by. He could see a face looking out at him, but before it passed by he saw a glint on the side of the road, and when the car was well past, he walked over to it and shined the flashlight on the cell phone. The bastard threw the phone out of the car.

"We're back to square one," said Poet.

"Back to the club," said Simon.

They drove slowly back to the strip club while

listening to the police scanner. There was a report of shots fired at Dreamers. Three squad cars were on the way. Off in the distance they could see the blue lights dancing on the surrounding buildings and powerlines.

They pulled into an empty parking lot a quarter mile away and watched with binoculars.

A small crowd of people were outside the club, police were talking with individuals, making their reports. Guaranteed there were more than a few people who didn't want to be seen. Car started to pull out, first a few, then more until the place was nearly deserted.

"There she is," said Simon as a distinct brunette walked out one of the side doors. A dark blue sedan was parked right next to the door and that club door had barely closed behind her when she was racing away from it, off towards the city.

Simon was ready. He pulled out onto the empty side street with his lights off, then turned them on as he got closer to traffic, blending in well behind her car. He had his window down so he could the sounds of engines around him.

She zig zagged down streets, through traffic lights in the slow lane, under freeways and overpasses, and train tracks, then when it seemed as though they were getting closer to the ocean, the smell of salt air wafting through the window, she pulled over in front of a three story apartment building, pink or orange in color, it was hard to tell at this hour before dawn.

Simon found a parking spot far behind her, and turned off his lights. She stayed in her car for a few minutes and they were wondering if she was even going to get out, when she finally opened the car door, thin ankles followed by long legs and a tight black dress, walking slow at first then quickly towards the mostly dark building.

A few long minutes went by and they saw a light in the top floor corner apartment. The drapes were open and she went over and closed them, looking furtively out the window as though she could see them watching. They could see the flash of her dark eyes, brooding under sharp narrow eyebrows.

Simon looked at the glow of his watch. It was four-thirty in the morning. A hell of a time to be getting home from work.

"Well, here we are on stake-out again," said Simon. "How's that arm?"

"Still attached. I think I'll live."

"You want to take a look at it with a flashlight?"

"Naw, I'm okay, just got a little nick on top."

"Can you make a fist?"

Poet bunched his hand into bare knuckles the size of a softball, and punched his open hand with a loud pop.

"Okay, you're good. I'll take the first shift and wake you up in an hour."

Poet mumbled and laid his head against the corner of the side window and was fast asleep. Within a few minutes he was breathing heavy and Simon wished he would have sent him into the back seat first but it was too late now and adjusted the side and rear view mirrors so he could see any movement around or behind the car, put earbuds in his ears and turned on Mozart to block out the snoring.

At six thirty the light in the apartment went on again for a couple of minutes, then went dark again. Simon woke up Poet. Candace came walking out of the apartment and got in her car and drove away, with Simon following.

She crisscrossed through town and stopped in front of a Catholic church and went inside. It was seven AM.

"We've got about an hour," said Simon.

They backtracked to the apartment, went up to the second floor, picked the lock of her apartment and got to work. Simon hid a camera in the living room while Poet hid one in the kitchen.

They searched the apartment, looking for clues. They weren't hard to find. Two photo albums were open on the coffee table. There was a wedding photo in the first album, and pictures of a baby girl in the other. Simon flipped through the albums and used his phone to take pictures of the different people. The wedding photos were the most intriguing. She was married to a tough looking Chinese Mexican dude with tattoos up and down his arms. He was wearing a shirt with short sleeves as though showing off the tats. In a couple of the wedding photos was a familiar face.

Leo.

It seemed like he was always lurking in the background, eyes never forward, but watching the edges of the party, like a bodyguard looking for trouble.

Simon punched into a facial recognition database and inserted the grooms picture.

"Tang Tang Fernandez, current residence Lompoc penitentiary.

"Time," said Poet as he looked at his watch. They'd been in the apartment twenty minutes.

Back at the car Simon opened up the laptop and pulled up the cameras and synched them.

Fifteen minutes later Candace returned to the apartment, went to the kitchen and made a bowl of cereal, they could see a rosary clutched in her hand and she placed it on the table as she sat down to eat.

The street in front of the apartment was getting busy as people got up and went to work. Cars left by the dozens. On the other side of the street a black sedan with tinted windows pulled up and parked. Out stepped a bald head attached to a burly frame. Leo.

Poet and Simon instinctively slid down into their seats with just the tops of their eyes looking over the dashboard. Leo seemed to be on a mission and he walked quickly across the street and into the apartment building.

Simon handed a small round tracker to Poet who got out, walked calmly across the street and down the sidewalk till he was next to the black sedan, pretended to drop something, then put the tracker under the back bumper and kept walking straight for a few car lengths before heading back to their car, looking down at his phone as though he was oblivious to the outside world.

Simon's laptop had a split screen with the kitchen camera on the right and the living room on the left. The volume was turned up and they could hear Leo talking to her, his back was to the living room camera while his face was towards the kitchen.

"Who were those two guys in the club last night?"

"How should I know? I've never seen them before in my life."

"They tagged my phone and followed me there, and then one of them seemed to recognize you. The tall one with the short hair who came up to you and threw all the money at your feet."

"I'm telling you the truth."

"He seemed to take a liking to you."

"A lot of men do. What do you expect in a strip club. I'm taking my clothes off for them."

Leo stepped quickly to his left towards her and punched her in the back of the head. They could hear the pop of knuckles on skull. She bounced against the stove with her hair flying into her face, then leaned forward pulling open a drawer and brandishing a butter knife in her right hand while brushing hair from her face.

Half fear, half burning anger in her eyes.

Leo laughed. "I could get used to this. Make sure you're at the club tonight on time."

Then he turned and walked out of the apartment, down to his car and drove off.

Poet waited a few minutes then started the car and followed.

Simon watched the camera as Candace got ice from the freezer, put it in a plastic baggie and set it against the back of her head where Leo had punched her. She lay down on the couch, curled into a fetal ball and closed her eyes. Within a few minutes she jerked unconsciously and then lay still again, sound asleep.

On the laptop computer screen there were two windows. One with Candace sound asleep, and the other a map of the city with a red dot in the center. The tracking device on the back of Leo's car. "The dot's not moving," said Simon. "His car's parked. Twenty fourth and Elm. It's two blocks away."

21.

Leo watched as the man came through the front door and walked through the restaurant towards the back table. He was wearing a black leather cowboy hat with the edges pulled down to shade his face even inside the restaurant which was weird.

Leo was calm, his eyelids drooping slightly as he took in the scene. The man walking towards him however was on edge, his eyes darting icily on the perimeter, looking for danger. He sat down opposite Leo and spread his hands on the table. The waitress came over and filled the plastic water glass with ice water while smiling.

"Just a coffee thanks," said the man as he took off the hat and laid on the side near the window, his eyes locked onto Leo's.

"Well?" said the man impatiently as though he were speaking to a child.

Leo slid an envelope across the table and the man looked down at it, then back up to Leo.

"What the hell is this?"

"Your payment."

"Some kind of a joke?"

"Open it up."

The man tapped on the envelope. It was flat and obviously empty.

"My deal with Tang Tang is a hundred thousand. Is there a hundred thousand dollar bill in here?"

Leo was unsmiling.

"Check it out."

The man opened it up and looked inside. Empty. He crumpled it up and rolled it back across the table.

"That's how we felt when we met the ship at the dock," said Leo. "We were supposed to meet up with an ex-Army Ranger with half a million in cash and ten pounds of heroin. We went to all that trouble, stuck our necks out, and imagine our surprise to find out someone else got there before us. I paid my support team out of my own pocket. I went home empty handed."

"That's your problem not mine. My deal with Tang was information, pure and simple. I provide the tip, and you take it from there. Fifty grand cash regardless whether you're successful or not. I made that very clear with him in the very beginning."

"Not this time."

"Then there won't be a next time."

Leo slid a picture of the man sitting next to Candace in the car, her tongue was on the edge of his ear.

"I'm caring less and less about that. My wife left me over a year ago."

Leo pulled out his phone and laid it on the

table, then pushed a button. It was recording from just a few moments ago.

"My deal with Tang Tang is a hundred thousand."

Leo punched the button again ending the playback.

"It's up in the cloud now."

"You bastard."

"It's true," said Leo. "My father, whoever in the hell he is or was, left my mother right before I was born. We've still got the ship coming into Long Beach in five days and if we're successful you'll get your money, and then we'll want another tip. How about that?"

The man's eyes hardened on the edges as he picked up his hat and got slowly out of the booth.

"Well don't be late this time."

22.

Simon and Poet watched from a distance, both with binoculars tight to their eyelids. They watched as the man with the black ten gallon cowboy hat strolled into the restaurant and went straight to the back table and sat in front of Leo.

Their heads barely moved but they were obviously talking about something, even at this distance you could see the tense body language.

The back of the man with the hat was turned away from them, but they could see Leo's lips moving. He pushed an envelope across the table, and a few moments later the other man opened it, crumpled it up and pushed it back across the table. There was an obvious conflict.

An empty envelope that was probably supposed to be filled with money. The man got up, put the hat back on his head and leaned down to tell something to Leo, then turned and walked back towards the entrance and out the door.

"I can't see his face, can you?"

"No," said Simon. "You stay here and I'll

follow him, we don't want people calling the cops if they see you wandering around with a bloody bandage on your arm."

Simon got out of the car, put his sunglasses on and started walking quickly down the sidewalk next to all the parked cars. The man with the black hat was also walking quickly away and down the opposite street, and had a two hundred yard head start.

"If I start running to catch up," thought Simon, "I'll attract too much attention." And he lengthened his stride while trying to appear natural.

The man took off his hat, got into the driver's side of a new white town car with dark tinted windows, sleek and low with fat black tires. It was an unmarked police car. It pulled out into traffic right in front of a car that had to slow down or rear-end him.

Simon pulled out the binoculars and tried to read the license plate but the car behind it was blocking his view. He turned to see their car parked down the street and thought about jogging back, but he locked eyes with Poet in the driver's seat, and motioned with his hand, then started walking quickly again, straining to watch the unmarked cop car disappear in the distance.

Poet pulled up next to him and Simon jumped in the passenger seat. "Straight ahead, white unmarked cop car, it's at the light."

"I see it."

Poet gunned the engine and passed a car on the left, zig zagging down the road to make up some distance. Two cars honked at him, then he was within ten cars of the unmarked.

"It's a cop," said Simon. "Imagine that."

"You see the color of the hat? It was black."

"Yeah," said Simon. "He's a bad cop."

"Now why is that," wondered Poet. "In all the movies. In all the stories. Why is the guy with the white hat the good guy, and the guy with the black hat the bad guy?"

"We're talking about hats Poet, not people. Most of those guys wearing the black hat in the old movies were white weren't they?"

Poet remained silent, musing as he drove.

They passed a few more cars and got within five cars of the unmarked, then Poet got into cruise mode. He could just see the edge of the white car as it travelled steadily down the road, then a few minutes later it turned right onto a four lane boulevard.

"This place look familiar to you?" asked Simon.

It was the police precinct where they got their marching orders just two days ago.

Poet slowed down so he wasn't too close as he made the turn. The unmarked turned right again into a driveway that led under the giant building into an underground parking garage.

The unmarked went through a metal gate that closed behind it.

"Let me out here and you go find a place to park," said Simon.

He jumped out of the car before it could stop all the way and pretended to look at his watch while taking in the entire area around him while Poet continued down the road.

Simon walked up to the edge of the driveway, and looked up at the clouds, smiling at them, a tourist on vacation, or a happy go lucky dumbass who just liked to walk around and look at clouds, non-threatening as he meandered up the driveway towards the metal gate. He could see the cameras positioned on the top corners of the roof, looking down on him. He wanted to wave, but looked at his watch again as though he were late for a meeting, or waiting for someone to meet him.

He walked up to the edge of the building and leaned against it, a loiterer, while he folded his arms and made his body as still as a statue, as still as the building he was leaning against.

From the corner of the gate he peered into the dark garage, it was cool like an air-conditioner from all the deep thick concrete and the air that flowed out from the belly of it smelled of tires and oil. He couldn't see any red tail lights from the car they were following, he was much too late for that, but straight through the center he could barely make out the elevator as the doors silently closed. Then the dimly lit number one turned into a number two and stopped.

Second floor.

Simon unfolded his arms and walked steadily past the building. No longer a tourist, he was on business, and needed to get to an appointment.

Poet was parked in front of the building, he'd found a spot that still had some time left on the meter and was watching him in the rear view mirror.

Simon got into the car.

"Remember how Finke said he wanted people to see us and wonder who we are? Well maybe it's time to go back up make ourselves be seen again."

"Did you get a look at the guy?"

"I was too late. But I saw the elevator stopped on the second floor."

"What room number?"

Simon gave Poet an malevolent eye.

"It didn't show me that wise guy. You stay in the car, and I'll go take a look around."

"How come you always get to go poking around and I'm stuck in the car?"

"I'm not the guy with the bloody arm. Next time don't get shot."

Poet looked at his right arm wrapped in the makeshift bandage.

"Good advice."

Simon started unloading his pockets, placing the items on the floor in front of him, Glock, billy club, mace, handcuffs, then got out of the car and headed to the stairs that led up to the double glass doors of the precinct.

23.

The two guards manning the entrance inside the doors recognized Simon walked in.

"Simon Profit NYPD," said the man sitting at the table with the notepad. He seemed pleased with himself, proud that he could remember someone's name that he only saw once, and wanted to show off his recollection prowess.

"That's right," said Simon as he pulled out his ID and placed it on the table.

"Are you carrying any weapons?"

"None today, I'm feeling pretty safe in this fine city you have here." He held his hands out palms open.

"What's your business sir?"

"I'm here to see Lieutenant Finke."

The guard wrote on the pad and motioned Simon through the metal detecting gate, then the guard on the other side waved the wand halfheartedly up and down Simon's sides, and nodded as he went through.

"Okay," he said simply and waited for the next customer.

It was busier today and the guards didn't seem to have time to shoot the breeze with an out of state cop. A stack of people waited in line to go through the gate and Simon was in, walking steadily to the stairs and up. Rubber running shoes screeching on the stairs. Turned left at the top down the hallway, the door to room 201 was closed so he walked past it to end of the hallway, strolling casually, most of the doors were closed but a few were open and he made sure to glance inside as he passed, and nodded as a courtesy to anyone who looked up from their work. Mostly it was men with sleeves rolled up and staring down at a pile of papers or a computer screen. No one looked as though they'd just gotten to the office, and there were no black cowboy hats in view. He turned at the end of the hall and went back to room 201.

Through the pale glazed glass he could see a shadow of movement, a body moving from right to left. He knocked politely.

"Come in," said a voice.

He was sitting at his desk, but it was obvious that he hadn't been a moment ago, he pulled a stack of papers from the corner of the desk to the center then looked up, surprise on his face though he tried not to show it.

"What are you doing here?"

"I needed to have a talk."

"You could have called, it's a heck of a lot more efficient."

"I don't trust electronics. I tap them for a living you know."

"You're supposed to be undercover."

"You said you wanted people to see us coming through the front door."

"Once. I wanted you to do that one time and then disappear. You may be jeopardizing the entire operation by showing back up here. You know that don't you?"

"I wanted to ask you about Fred Pillar."

Finke took a deep breath and sighed.

"Yeah, that was a heck of thing to happen. Hotheaded road rage in a church parking lot of all places."

"We got there after the incident, we saw his body. He was shot in the back."

"Yes, I know, I saw the report. You got there about half an hour after the incident. What were you doing there?"

"We were supposed to meet for breakfast, he didn't show up, he told us where he was going so we checked it out."

"You interviewed a witness, something about a Camaro. It's in the report. You shouldn't have butted in. Now *you're* in the report."

"We told them we just met and were here for the police convention on crowd control. Just like you told us to do."

Finke remained silent, tapping his forefinger on the desk. This conversation was going nowhere and needed to end.

"Did they find the car?" asked Simon.

"As a matter of fact they did, or think they did. It was burned to a crisp under the freeway."

"Did they ID it?"

"VIN number was filed off, it's a dead-end. Drop it Profit."

Treating him like a child. Telling him to go sit in the corner and be quiet.

"Any other leads?" asked Simon. "I'm just curious of course. He was our partner, if even for just one day."

"You know how this works. Homicide has the case, and they're usually hush-hush about any leads or evidence they might have. But from what I understand it's looking like a random act of passion and they have no real leads."

"Do they know about us, I mean Poet and myself and you."

By his body language Finke was tiring of the questioning and his reply was dry.

"They do not. I was able to see the report as a matter of courtesy since he was assigned to my division for a future project yet to be determined. As you and Poet are. How is he by the way?"

"Just peachy. He's getting plenty to eat and lots of rest and I make sure to tuck him in at night and I even sing him a lullaby to make sure he sleeps well."

That agitated Finke. He was silent but Simon could see the anger brewing inside. Finally he stopped tapping his finger and pointed it across the table at Simon.

"Now listen to me detective Profit. I brought you in here for a specific job. You lost a partner and that is a bona fide tragedy, but unfortunately that happens quite often in our line of work. Now are you here to give me your resignation, or are you going back out there to do your job, either way make up your mind, because I have other tasks to take care of. This is a big city and crime never rests. Ever."

Simon got up and smiled politely.

"Sorry lieutenant, we don't know each other that well, and probably never will. I guess the thought of trying to nail scumbags on the street and maybe getting shot for the effort makes me a cynical man with a twisted sense of humor if you can call it that."

He turned to go out the door and stopped to admire the wall lined with pictures, and awards.

Full festooned formal uniformed men and women at banquets receiving awards on a stage, every day uniformed cops with earmuffs and safety glasses at target ranges posing with pistols and rifles, cops posing with politicians, cops posing with children at sporting events, cops in a parade riding a horse.

There was even a small picture of a man on a horse somewhere in the desert, it could have been anywhere in the world or maybe even just west of Los Angeles, tumbleweeds and tall cactus, the man posing in the saddle while cradling a rifle in his arms, wearing a black cowboy hat.

Simon's eyes lingered on the picture for just a moment too long, he was shocked in a way and tried to cover it up by looking back at some of the other pictures.

"Well, I won't take up any more of your time."

Simon looked back over at Finke who was studying him. There's a certain glare that emanates from a man's eyes when he distrusts what he sees, a fear of being outed, an uncovered dirty lie exposed, and that's the glare that Simon saw in Finke's eyes.

He was the man with the black hat.

There's also a look that emanates from a man who's suddenly confronted with pure evil, who knows that the evil one is going to burn in hell forever, who even has pity in some ways that what will be will be, that the retribution that is coming though well-deserved could have easily been avoided by simply doing the right thing, and that's the look that emanated from Simon's eyes as he watched Finke.

Then he turned and walked out the door without another word.

24.

Simon walked down the concrete steps one at a time, calmly descending to street level. On the back of his head he could feel eyeballs, Finke's eyeballs drilling into his skull.

He got to the little sedan, opened the passenger door and buckled his seatbelt.

"Drive," he said simply, and Poet started the car and pulled away from the curb.

"What'd you find out?"

"We're gonna need another car."

"Why?"

"Because this one is marked."

"I've been sitting here the whole time. No one put a tracer on us."

"The license plate, we're tagged. Turn right here, then left."

"What are you talking about?"

"You know how sometimes you get a weird feeling that something aint quite right?"

"Yeah. All the time. Like right now in fact."

"Well I should have felt it the moment I walked into Finke's office the very first time. But

I guess our little banter about race and Shakespeare threw me off the scent."

"Man you are babbling."

"I should have known there was something wrong about that guy. Turn right here."

Poet cut in front of an old lady and she honked her horn at him and gave him the finger.

They were on a four lane highway heading west into the sunset. Simon saw far up ahead what he was looking for, a line of taxis in front of a restaurant.

"Pull in here and park," he said pointing to an open space along the curb. He reached into the back seat and pulled out a back pack rummaging through it and pulled out a long sleeve jacket.

"Here wear this, don't want anyone to get suspicious of your bloody arm."

"What in the hell is going on Simon?" Poet was no dummy. "It's Finke isn't it?"

"We were having a nice little conversation, until I saw the picture of him on a horse wearing a black cowboy hat."

"Lots of people have black cowboy hats. Tell me you have something besides a picture of a guy wearing a hat."

"It wasn't really the hat as much as the look in his eye when I saw it. You know that look?"

Poet nodded. "You mean the look that you get when you catch a kid with his hand in the cookie jar?"

"Something like that."

"It's the same look, only as they get older and the crime gets a little more serious, the look stays the same, only grimmer. When they're a kid they still have a glint of innocence, and as they get older that glint is gone."

"That's the look. I think you need more than a picture of a hat to put a guy on the gallows."

Simon looked around through the glove compartment and under the seats to make sure they didn't leave anything. Then pulled a shirt out his backpack and wiped down the steering wheel and door handles.

"It's clean, let's go."

"Really?" said Poet. "My car's a crime scene?"

"This is the business we're in," said Simon. "We still don't know who we're dealing with. Ideally we should fire-bomb the interior and get rid of all of the evidence that we were here, every hair follicle and flake of skin. In case they decide to use it in a real crime and implicate us. Let's go."

They walked to the line of cabs and got in the back seat of the one in front.

"Fourth and main," said Simon.

The cab driver looked at the two men sitting in the back seat and nodded.

"Okay." Then he radioed in his location and the destination to an operator, adjusted the mirrors, pushed the button on the meter and got ready to pull out from the curb. An unmarked police car, white with dark tinted windows and fat black tires came down the boulevard passing on the other side and slowed down. The driver looking past the cab and on their side of the road. Both Simon and Poet wanted to look back to see where it was headed, but both knew without actually seeing with their own eyes.

They also didn't want to alert the cab driver that anything was wrong or out of the ordinary with them suddenly showing up for a cab ride.

When the driver hesitated from pulling out from the curb and looked at his rear view mirror with a concerned look in his eyes, both Simon and Poet asked him what was the hold-up.

"Somebody in trouble I think," came the driver's answer, and they both looked back. The unmarked had been joined by a patrol car with lights on top and they hemmed in the little white car down the block.

"Maybe some poor bastard parked too close to the curb," said Simon. "They should give the guy a break."

"I support our local police," said Poet. "I hope they throw the book at them."

The driver chuckled at that, took one more look in the side mirror then glanced to his left through the window and pulled away from the curb.

"Choo guys from out of town?" ventured the driver. Sometimes if you were friendly to the customers they gave you a tip.

"Naw, we're from Detroit," said Poet. "Here for the cop convention down at the civic center. You heard about it?"

"Oh yes sir," the driver lied.

25.

Simon's giant silver SUV was where they left it two days ago. Someone left an empty beer bottle on the bumper but other than that it looked in good shape.

He tossed the bottle into a trash can and threw the keys to Poet who deftly caught them with his good left hand.

"You wanna drive?"

"And deprive you of your pride and joy?"

"I can share."

"I've seen you frowning every time you get into the passenger side of my car. You may not have noticed it, but I sure as hell did."

"I was grimacing because I had to bend down far enough to get into the seat. I have a bad knee."

"Well you aint gonna see me grimace when I have to jack myself up into this hillbilly monster truck."

"Jump in and take off the jacket and the bandage. Let's take a look at your wound."

Simon pulled a metal case from under the

back seat, unlatched the locks and laid it open on his lap. It was filled with bandages, surgical equipment, sutures, a staple gun, ointments, washes, and drugs. Like a mini ER unit.

"Who in world carries all this stuff?" said Poet.

"Me, now take off the bandage." He put a flexible pan under Poets arm, and motioned for him to get moving.

Poet shook his head and did as he was told, but the cloth was stuck to the wound with dried blood and when he was finally able to peel it off, a fresh red stream began to flow.

Simon slowly poured liquid from a bottle into the wound to clean it and open it up. Poet winced a bit, drawing a sharp breath in between his teeth no matter how hard he tried not to.

"Does that hurt?" asked Simon.

"Hell yeah, what do you think?" said Poet looking closer at the wound. "Is that a bone."

"It's just a tendon, relax."

"Just a tendon..."

"You're going to need stitches."

"Okay then get me to a doctor."

"We don't have time for that."

Simon opened up a box and pulled out a curved needle and black thread.

"Don't tell me you're gonna try to do it."

"Relax, this isn't my first rodeo."

"Are you going to tell me you're also a doctor."

"No, I'm a registered nurse."

Poet almost choked and laughed out loud. He tried to stop laughing but it was singularly contagious and took a while for him to catch his breath.

"You son of a bitch, you crack me up. What college did you go to?"

Simon got out a syringe and started poking it along the wound. Poet cringed with every poke.

"Damn man!"

"Local anesthesia. The bullet made quite a little gully on top of your arm. Like someone put a little trenching machine to work. Gonna make a bitchin scar. The chicks will dig it. Too big of a gap for thread to pull it together though. This is gonna take staples. Stainless steel, they'll pull that gap closed in no time, and stay closed no matter what you do. I've actually been wanting to try this thing out for a long time but never had the need. So in a way this is all very fortuitous. Gotta look on the bright side you know. I think it's gonna take at least seven staples, maybe more."

He took out what looked like a battery operated screw driver and placed the tip against the inside of the wound zapping along the edges with an electric pulse, searing the wound, stopping the bleeding, then pulled out the medical staple gun and loaded a shiny curved staple into the end.

"C'mon man, what college did you go to for your nurses degree."

Simon didn't answer. With his free left hand squeezing the gully together and with the staple gun in the right hand, placing the tip at the beginning of the gully he snapped the gears and the staple clamped the skin shut. Poet let out a little groan and stayed still.

"Oh, I didn't actually go to college," said Simon.

Poet's face scrunched up, his bloodshot eyes ready to jump out of their sockets and destroy Simon.

"No," continued Simon as he loaded another staple in the gun, "I took an on-line course, it's just about the same."

Six clicks later and the wound was sealed.

"Let's get back to Leo. I think it's time we took him into custody."

"Agreed. Then we pay a little visit to Finke."

Simon opened the laptop and looked at the window with the red dot.

"He's still in the same place. Still at the restaurant."

But when they got back to the restaurant, Leo's car was gone.

"Something wrong with the tracker?" asked Poet. "Reboot the computer."

Simon did a quick re-boot, but the red dot on the satellite map still showed up on the street outside the middle window of the restaurant.

Simon got out and walked over next to the window and the tracker was stuck to a metal lamp post. He looked around at the buildings and alleyways surrounding them. Maybe Leo was somewhere watching. Tracking them now.

26.

"Back to square one," said Simon.

He drove to the street where Candace's apartment was located and parked two blocks away.

"Maybe Leo's an idiot and we'll get another shot at him."

"We had our chance," said Poet. "But if we grabbed him this morning, we wouldn't have found out about our buddy Finke. He aint coming back here, I'll bet he knows we put the tracker on him outside her apartment."

They sat in the SUV while watching the cameras in the apartment. Candace slept on the couch till after one o'clock, took a shower and got ready to go out. She was dressed simple, plain. If you didn't know any better you would never in your wildest dreams guess she was a stripper.

They followed her through the city streets until she stopped at a mall with a grocery store.

"I know," said Poet. "I'll wait here while you go 'check it out'."

"Finally got you trained."

"What's your plan?"

"Play it by ear I guess. Wait till she gets into an area that's open where she won't feel threatened. Walk up to her and calmly explain the situation. We need her help. Pure and simple."

"There is nothing pure and simple in this world. And you know it."

Simon got out of the car and walked towards the supermarket and went in through the front door and turned left, the normal route that most people took. There was a bread section, condiments, and towards the back was the fresh vegetables. He could see Candace standing in front of the apples. She picked one up, inspected it, turning over before placing it back in the pile, then picked up another to begin the process again, finally satisfied, she placed it in a plastic bag, then into the cart.

There was no sense playing around. He walked straight up to her and stood on the other side of the bin. Eight feet away with a pile of produce in between them, but still close enough for her to hear him.

"Good selection," he said.

She looked over her large black rimmed sunglasses at him, eyes narrowed for a moment with either animosity or recognition, he couldn't tell which. There was no mirth or happiness on the edges of those eyelids, and then they disappeared up and over the sunglasses as she moved to the next bin without a word in return and began to scan the peaches, picked one up, turned it over, gazing at the surface, then put it in a plastic bag and placed it in the cart with the single apple.

"Do you always buy just one?" he asked moving along on the other side of the bin.

"I'm not interested," she said and moved to the plums, picked one up, turned it over, and satisfied placed it in a plastic bag. Her attitude reserved and calm, moving slowly and methodically, disregarding all around her including Simon who moved with her on the other side of the bin, ignoring him. Consistent in her actions.

"I need to talk to you," he said.

"Should I call security?"

He pulled out his ID and badge and placed them on top of the pile of plums.

"You're a cop," she said.

"I was at the club last night," he said.

"I know. I saw you. So what?"

"I wasn't there for the show."

"Everyone's there for the show."

"Not me."

"So what were you there for?"

"I followed someone. I'm investigating a crime. It's what I do."

"What does this have to do with me?"

"I noticed your tattoo, the one on your ankle. A golden Aztec sun."

"It's not unusual. A lot of girls have them."

"I'm just looking for one particular girl that has it."

"What's particular about her?"

"She knows this person."

Simon pulled out his phone and showed her a picture of himself with Fred Pillar and Poet at the boxing ring. The selfie he took with Fred's grandpa. He noticed the muscles along her face slacken, her breath inhale slightly, a fight or flight response.

Flight it would be.

She turned and walked quickly towards the front of the store, towards the door.

He followed as fast as he could without causing anyone to notice.

She was out the door and moving towards the parking lot. He was able to close the distance and walk next to her as she made her way across the hot asphalt to her car.

"He was my partner," said Simon. "The crime I'm investigating is his murder in the parking lot at the Catholic Church two days ago."

"I can't help you," she said as she pulled keys from her purse and in one swift motion unlocked the car.

He reached out and gently held on to her elbow.

"Please," he asked her.

She turned towards him and equally as gently twisted her elbow out of his grasp. He noticed tears streaming down her cheeks from underneath the sunglasses.

"I can't," she whispered. "They'll kill her."

"Who?" he whispered back, mirroring her behavior.

Two men walking nearby noticed the interaction. Both of them burly construction workers covered in dust after a long day of work, probably heading to the store to buy a case of beer. The smaller of the two tapped his buddy on the shoulder and motioned for him to follow as he walked up to Simon.

"Hey pal, are you bothering this girl?" He reached out and set a paw on Simon's right shoulder.

"No I'm not," said Simon. "We're just having a private conversation."

The other bigger guy cornered Simon, standing next to his left shoulder.

"Then why's she crying?" said the bigger guy.

"You guys need to mind your own business," said Simon.

There was a hairline moment when the smaller of the two stepped back and got ready to throw a punch when all eyes instinctively went down to Candace and the familiar object she held in her hand, cradling it with precision next to her hip. A square nosed pistol aimed at the bigger guy's stomach. Time stood still as she spoke methodically.

"I'm crying because I'm happy, is that a crime? Now you two dudes need to go on your merry way and leave us alone, as the man said we're having a private conversation. Okay?"

"Okay lady, we just thought you were in trouble," said the big guy as he moved ever so slowly backwards, eyes on the barrel of the gun, then turned and continued on his not so merry way, face beet red, fear sweat streaming down his meaty face, walking towards the store followed close behind by his other nosy friend.

One case of beer might not be enough after

the encounter.

Candace put the gun back in her purse, took off her sunglasses and gazed at Simon's eyes, studying him as he unflinchingly gazed back at her.

"Do you have a car?" she asked.

"Right over there," he said, pointing to the giant SUV with Poet in the driver's side watching the whole event.

"That's the other guy in the picture that you showed me."

"Yes, that's Poetamos."

"Interesting name."

"He's my other partner."

"He was at the club last night."

"You have nice eyes," said Simon before he could correct himself. "I mean you have good eyes, great attention to details to notice him in the crowd is what I meant."

She was used to having men fall over their themselves around her and if this was a normal day with normal circumstances she might have managed a bit of a smile. But those days were long gone. She studied him for a few long moments more before making up her mind.

"Follow me," she said. "I know a place we can talk."

She got in her car and started it up before he could say a word and jogged back to the SUV and jumped into the passenger seat.

"Follow her," was all Simon said.

They drove behind her through a labyrinth of streets, a mixed up maze of residential and commercial district streets. It was almost as though she were trying to cast off a tail.

"You see anyone following us?" asked Simon as Poet maneuvered the SUV through traffic.

"No, but we stick out like a sore thumb in this giant vehicle. Someone could be lurking a mile away and we wouldn't even know it."

Candace took a right turn down a four lane boulevard then turned into a parking lot guarded by a rock gate.

It was a Catholic Church. The sign read Saint Barnabas.

She was already walking into the front door church when Poet pulled the SUV up to the curb.

"You want me to wait here?"

"No, come with me, let's see what she has to say."

It was quiet inside the cathedral, the air had a tinge of mold or dust, and echoes both real and perceived. A footstep reverberated up into the air and you could hear the sound bounce off a wall fifty feet away.

She was at the back left corner, kneeling in the pew in front of the seat head down as though she was deep in prayer with a white knitted shawl over her head.

Poet sat in the middle of the row in front of her and Simon walked down the line of seats and sat down next to her right elbow.

She lifted herself back into the seat and rolled the shawl back over her head and layered it around her shoulders. She seemed at peace, unlike in the parking lot at the store when she had the gun in her hand. Or when she was up on stage with no clothes dancing next to a pole with a mask on her face. Here, calmness and light seemed to emanate from her skin. Simon studied her expression. Her eyes were half closed and when she breathed in it seemed as though she was breathing in more than air, for air itself was barren and lifeless compared to the essence she was inhaling, it was as if she was breathing in all the prayers that had ever been said in this place, and exhaling them through her skin. Exuding some type of life that transcended life itself.

"I feel safe here," she said finally as she opened her eyes and turned to Simon. "No matter what happens in the world. This is a sanctuary."

Poet turned halfway to the left in his seat and nodded at her.

"Ma'am," he said politely.

"So you're Poetamos," she said.

He nodded simply.

"Yes, ma'am, that's me."

"Poet is here from San Francisco, and I'm from New York City. We were hired by the police department to work on a case down at the docks. Did Fred tell you anything about our work?"

She shook her head.

"I didn't even know he was in the police department. I didn't know anything about him. I guess you could say it was me that pursued him. In a way, that is. I sat down next to him one morning in a church much like this one, and it just felt right, so I continued to do so for many days. It was almost as though he was saving the seat for me. He would sit right where you are sitting, Simon Profit."

Simon motioned to the bag on her lap. The dull black metal handle of the gun was sticking slightly out of the top, ready to grab if needed.

"That was nifty move, pulling that gun on those two construction workers back at the store parking lot."

"A girl has to be ready to defend herself."

"You ever use it? The gun I mean."

"All the time. There's a range near my condo."

"I mean on a person."

"Not yet."

"Well let's hope you never have to."

Poet looked at Simon and tilted his head to get the conversation moving. They needed answers, not small talk. The implication was not lost on Candace.

"Tell me about Fred Pillar," she asked.

"Sure," said Simon. "He was born in East L.A., he grew up in Compton and a lot of other little towns around here, his parents moved just about every year and he had to adjust at a lot of different schools, he was always the new guy. Said he felt like a military brat. He went to Montebello High School, was a golden gloves boxer, he was working in Denver in the metro before getting hired here a few weeks before we showed up."

Poet nodded, marveling that Simon had remembered all that from the meeting they had at Finke's office the first time they met Fred.

"He was a golden gloves boxer?" asked Candace.

"Yeah," said Simon. There was no sense

dancing around it. "That's why we think it's strange that someone could get the jump on him..."

"And shoot him in the back," said Candace, finishing the sentence.

"Yeah," said Simon. "And be able to do that."

"We think a guy named Leo Andrade did it," said Poet.

"Oh no, I don't think he did it," said Candace, shaking her head and looking towards the front of the church towards the figure of the man on the cross. "I know he did it."

"We need your help to find him," said Simon. "How often does he come to the club?"

"Sometimes every night. Sometimes once a month. He disappears when he senses danger. After what happened last night I don't think we'll see him for a long time. He's like a snake in the grass, slithering along, sneaking around, then slinking into a hole in the ground."

She shook her head and looked towards the front of the church.

"You'll never find him."

Simon sighed and sat back in his chair while watching her. Watching the side of her face and her eyes fastened on the object at the front of the long hall. Eyes sharp and clear as crystal framed by long black eyelashes. She turned her attention from the front of the church towards him and stared into his eyes. It was the kind of moment that might happen once in a person's life if you were lucky enough and were paying attention. You can't plan for it. Can't force it to happen with one-sided will. Can't train your instincts to be on the lookout for it. Some people call it a spark, a thunderbolt, an ethereal combustion between two people that can't be defined. It either happens or it doesn't, and for just about every single person in the entire world that has ever lived it never, ever happens.

From Simon's perspective, not once had he ever seen a woman look at him like this. The intense warmth of her dark eyes stunned him to silence. Normally in control, ready to take action at a moment's notice, or with no warning at all, ready to jump into a fight without thinking of the consequences, he was suddenly without a single thought in his brain, as though the only real thing in the world was the vision he was watching with his eyes.

From her perspective she saw an intense pragmatic man, her polar opposite and yet the same deep spirit encased in ice blue eyes, as though she could jump right in and swim in them, a surreal cobalt mix of calm color and emotion, an aquatic sanctuary surrounded by granite rough eyebrows and face. Someone she could trust. Someone that could help her. Someone she could help. With one single look a partnership was formed without words.

Poet, from his perspective was the odd man out, as though neither one of them even realized that he was still here just a few feet away, as though in some separate world he didn't exist.

There was a noise at the back of the church as a old couple came shuffling through the front door. They looked to the left as they walked, nodding acknowledgement to the trio sitting in the back of the church, then they continued on down the aisle to the front pews, crossed themselves and sat down well out of earshot.

Their trance was broken. Both blinked and regained composure. There was a task at hand. A job that needed to be completed.

"You were saying we'll never find Leo," said Poet.

"I have a husband, his name is Tang Tang Fernandez, and he's in prison in Lompoc for assaulting a police officer."

"We know that," said Simon.

She nodded. Of course they did.

"You may think you know everything about me, but I'm going to tell you anyways. I have a daughter with Tang Tang," said Candace. "Her name is Belina, she is two and a half years old and is the most beautiful thing in this entire world to me. When I told Tang I was leaving him, he had Leo kidnap Belina and take her away. I get a picture of her every week. They are holding her hostage. He doesn't care about me, or about Belina. To him we are possessions. Objects. Tools to be used. Things of value, and when that value is used up, we can be discarded. I have no illusions that he would have us both killed if our value is gone. What man kidnaps his child and uses her to force his wife to work in a strip club? His own beautiful child."

She lowered her head and wiped away a tear, then steeled her nerves and looked at Simon.

"But they made a mistake and now I know where she is."

"Then let's go get her."

She shook her head.

"Not with Leo lurking in the shadows somewhere, ready to jump out of a bush in the middle of the night. We'd never be safe."

"He can't stay hidden forever," said Poet. "We found him once, we'll find him again."

"I have an idea," she said. "I think I know how we can flush him out. But it will put myself and Belina in great danger. Myself I don't mind, but my daughter... I have a feeling that we may have one chance to save her."

27.

Cordell rapped his baton on the metal bars of the cells as he walked down the corridor on the second floor of the prison.

When he got in front of Tang Tang's cell he just stood there and watched as the man with tattoos up and down his arms and across his back did pushups, bare hands on concrete floor, ropes of muscles covered in sweat writhing under pressure, a moving tapestry of living graffiti art, sharp etched black ink on brown skin contorting, twisting, warping, deforming with each fluid movement. He heard the wood baton on metal as it made its way towards his cell and he could see the shiny black boots at the corner of his eye, but he needed to get his numbers and when he finished with the fiftieth consecutive push-up, he climbed to his feet and looked out the bars.

"What do you want?" he said to the guard.

"It's your wife," said Cordell. "She called. Said she needs to talk to you. Says it's an emergency."

"What happened?"

"She wouldn't tell the operator. Said she needed to talk to you and only you. Let's go."

Tang Tang hadn't talked to Candy in over a year. It was their deal. His deal actually. He didn't want to talk to her, not while he was in prison. He had no control over a conversation while he was stuck behind bars. He couldn't reach out and smack her across the mouth if she talked back to him. She was in control.

"What if I don't want to talk to her?" he said.

"It's up to you. She sounded pretty upset. Or so the operator said. She said she'd call back in exactly twenty minutes. That was ten minutes ago. I can get you down to the phone bank in time. If you want."

Tang Tang squinted his eyes. He was suspicious. Wary. And yet intrigued. There was only one way to find out what she wanted. He pulled on the grey shirt and tucked it into his pants. It was instantly blotted with sweat on all sides. A human Rorschach stain. The guard opened the cell door and he walked slowly in front of the guard down the hallway to the stairs.

28.

Poet drove the SUV down the freeway to the third exit in Cerritos, under the highway and over a dry river bed heading north. A small single engine turbo prop flew low overhead in front of them on its approach to the airport.

Ten minutes later they turned onto Calente Avenue, and parked two doors down from the white house with the black metal numbers 401 nailed above the garage.

There was a black sedan in the driveway. The front door was open and they could see the TV set on in the living room. A cartoon was on the screen.

"Man, I don't like this," said Poet. "It's too dangerous for the child. Looks all pretty and nice and neat, but this is a hostage situation. Let's call in a professional team who are trained and equipped for this type of operation."

"No," said Candace. "That's how she gets hurt and you never find Leo."

"Don't forget about Finke," said Simon. "Would you trust anyone right about now and call in for back-up."

"You got a point. I just don't like it, okay?"

"You ready?" asked Simon.

It took a moment for her to react, but then Candace nodded. "Yeah."

She pulled out the square nosed pistol from her purse and checked the clip again for the tenth time in the past half hour, nervous that she might somehow find it empty.

Simon was serious as he looked at her.

"We have to time this perfectly. You walk in front of me, straight through the door and sit down next to Belina. Don't announce your presence, don't say her name. Don't pull out that weapon for any reason. That's why I'm here. If there's any trouble, I'll take care of it. Poet's our back-up, he'll stay here in the car with the engine running. We pick up Belina like we're going to take her to a birthday party and get her back in this car. And then I'll wait for what's coming. Poet will take you to the motel and get you set up and then come back for me. Hopefully I'll have Leo in custody."

Poet laid his revolver on the floor next to his foot.

Candace punched the phone number to the prison in Lompoc.

"This is Candace Fernandez, I spoke with someone earlier about talking to my husband Tang Tang. Yes, I'll wait."

Poet looked at Simon. "You think they'd ping the phone to find our location?"

"I would because I don't need a warrant. But they do."

Candace was calm on the outside, but Simon could see tension rising in her face as she waited. A slight twitch along the right eyebrow, nostrils flaring on the edges with an increase in breath volume.

She put the phone on speaker. A moment later the receiver on the other end clicked and a man's voice came on the line.

"Who's there?"

"Candace."

"Why are you calling? What happened."

"Nothing yet," she said. Her voice trembled on the edges.

"What do you mean yet. Are you threatening me bitch?"

It was as though a switch was clicked from on to off in her outer appearance. Her psyche. The twitch at the corner of her eye smoothed to calm resolve, the tremble in her voice disappeared, replaced by cool force and determination.

"I know where Belina is. I know where you took her."

Silence at the other end.

Then.

"Bullshit."

She nodded, the edges of her mouth crinkled as she very slightly smiled. It was the answer she wanted.

"I know where she is Tang, and I'm going to get her and bring her home."

"You're not gonna do shit, you damned whore, tú puta. Tú perra loca, crazy bitch."

"You're going to leave us alone, or I'll go to the police. I'll turn state's evidence against you."

"For what? I'm innocent."

"Murder, extortion, kidnapping."

"None of it's true."

"You've been bribing a cop for the past two years. You used me."

"I don't know what you're talking about," said Tang Tang. He knew the line was tapped. "You're bluffing."

"Calente Avenue," she whispered into the phone. "I'm heading there now, and there's nothing you can do to stop me." She pressed the red button to end the call and looked at Simon.

"Let's go," she said.

They got out of the car and walked towards the house. As they got to the front door they could hear the phone inside ringing.

Tang Tang, in the prison call center looked at the silent phone after Candace hung up, eyes narrowing in anger, veins throbbing at the side of his forehead. From memory he dialed the phone number of Leo's grandmother in Cerritos. The phone rang five times before she picked up and he spoke quickly and efficiently in Spanish to her.

"Verna, es Belina's papa."

"Tang Tang?" she said.

He could sense surprise in her voice since he had never once called while he'd been in prison. In fact the instructions she'd been given were if he ever did call, then something was wrong.

"Where's Belina?" he asked.

"Right here watching cartoons. What's wrong?"

"Nothing," he said, trying to diffuse the fear, the panic in her voice. "Pack a small bag and take her on a little vacation for a day or two. Leave the door to the house open. Leave in the next five minutes, understood?"

"Yes Tang," she said then heard the phone on the other end tap out.

Tang Tang dialed another number and waited while it rang and rang. He wanted to slam the phone against the wall when there was no answer but that would bring trouble.

He tried dialing another number and got the same result.

He pulled a piece of paper out of his pocket and reluctantly dialed a third number.

It rang once and was answered with silence on the other end.

"Candy called me," said Tang Tang. "She's going to take Belina. How soon can you be there?"

"Ten minutes," said the voice on the other end, then hung up.

Simon held the gun low at his side while he looked through the screen door. The old woman hung up the phone and went into the bedroom.

He could hear her shuffling things around. He gently pushed his thumb into the door latch on the handle. It was unlocked and it opened silently. Candace followed her into the front hallway. Sitting on the floor enraptured in the colorful cartoon characters, was a small girl with jet black hair.

Candace walked silently into the living room, while holding the pistol in her right hand and sat gently next to her. The small girl's face turned slowly, her eyes and mouth went wide as she saw her mother and she was about to squeal out when Candace placed her index finger over Belina's mouth and shook her head.

"Shhhh," she whispered. She picked up her baby and headed around the sofa towards the front door.

"Belina?" came the voice from the bedroom and the old lady came out with a knitted shawl over her shoulders and arms that hung down past her knees. She saw Simon standing in the doorway with the pistol in his hand, barrel pointing up.

She was an old woman who looked around seventy or eighty years old with pure grey hair that cascaded down around her shoulders, tired wrinkled eyes and a confused look on her face as she looked at the intruder in her house with the gun in his hand. Then she saw Candace holding Belina near the sofa, and saw the gun in her hand also.

Too late Simon saw the subtle movement.

The shawl dropped off the shoulders revealing the hands that gripped the sawed off shotgun. The tired old woman moved swiftly for someone her age, the double barreled shotgun rotated up and over, blasting a shot that took out the corner of the wall and nicked Simon in the hip. He dove out of the way of the second barrel while she crouched and swiveled towards Candace who also lunged for cover pushing Belina behind the couch in front of her.

The old woman crouched and shuffled towards the couch with the shotgun ready at her hip.

"Come out you damn whore," she whispered. "Drop the gun and show your face, or I'll kill the baby."

In the corner of her eye she saw Simon at the corner of the wall again. Too late. He took quick aim and fired at her forearm hitting her below the elbow, knocking the shotgun out of her hands.

The old lady was tough as gristle and rolled over the gun getting ready to pick it up again, she had one hand on the barrel and the other groping towards the trigger when Candace came around the sofa with the square nosed pistol and put a bullet in between her eyes, then stood there for a moment looking down at the ruffled pile of grey hair with the dark pool of red black liquid spreading throughout it, the grey head jerked twice and was still.

Belina was crying behind the sofa. She hadn't seen what happened and Candace was determined not to let her see it. She rounded the couch, picked her up swiftly with one hand cradling her in the nook of her elbow holding her tight to her shoulder and went out the door into the sunlight. She slid the pistol into her front pocket and walked towards the SUV with Poet in the driver's side with the engine idling.

As she got into the back seat with Belina, still holding her tight, as soon as the door was closed, "Go," she said, and he pulled away from the curb and headed down the road.

No one poked their heads from their doors, not one single concerned neighbor walked towards the house.

"Sounded like a car backfired," said Poet. "Then two balloons popped."

Candace and Belina sat quietly in the back seat, holding each other.

"I think Simon is hurt," she said. "But the old woman is dead."

29.

Simon lifted his shirt and unbuckled his pants to see a chunk of meat ripped from the top of his hip. It looked like a big dog had taken a bite out of him. Blood welling in the cavity. He went to the kitchen and grabbed the roll of paper towels sitting on the counter, wadded up a bunch, pressed it against the wound then pulled his trousers tight against it, cinching the belt, applying pressure like a tourniquet. It would have to do.

He worked fast, opened the bag with the gear. He took the four motion detectors and put one at each side of the house, taping them to the window facing out, one stun grenade hidden on the floor under each window. If he got into a running battle within the house he wanted options.

Two identical Glock 17's on each hip and one nestled in his right hand. He had to wait till Leo came into the house. It had to be done inside.

There was less chance Leo could slip away. Sure it was more dangerous to bring him close in, but that's the way it had to be. Like trapping a lion while waiting inside the trap itself.

The kitchen was the center of the house and so he stayed there with the motion detecting monitor on the floor beneath the counter. It was designed to detect people, not cars or animals. Human beings.

The glass face of the microwave hanging under the cabinet over the stove faced the living room where the old woman lay still. From his position in the kitchen Simon could see the couch in the reflection.

Simon estimated five minutes had elapsed since the old woman pulled the sawed off shotgun out from under her shawl. The neighborhood was silent with only the occasional car passing by. The second hand on the clock on the wall clicked lightly as it travelled around the edges.

The motion detector at the rear window facing the back yard lit up on the monitor, a black flashing light. Simon crouched behind the counter. The sound of a screen door lightly opening. No audible vibrations of a person, but the volume of air displaced by something.

Simon could see in the microwave reflection a bald head moving towards the living room, and so he moved towards the edge of the wall with the Glock at arm's length.

Leo's back was to the kitchen as he rounded the couch and the moment he caught sight of the old woman, he jumped down into a squat, pistol up and ready.

Simon tossed a stun grenade from the kitchen

into the middle of the living room. In the corner of his eye Leo caught sight of the projectile, following its flight path over his head, fired two shots into the kitchen and rolled over the dead woman as the grenade exploded, then leaped through the air crashing through a window into the back yard.

"Damn," whispered Simon as he fired two shots through the wall beneath the broken window then rushed over to the back of the house peering along the edge of another window. Two quick pops from outside and glass showered over Simon's head.

Leo was trying to climb over the fence at the back of the house. Simon fired a quick shot at Leo's feet as he leaped over to the other side.

Simon sprinted to the back screen door and plowed through it. He could see the top of Leo's bald head moving fast across the neighbor's back yard heading to the front and pure adrenalin kicked in. Bolting towards the back fence, scrambling over it and then running down the side of the house he could see Leo getting into the black sedan he'd left parked on the street.

Out into the front yard Simon fired quickly blowing out the passenger side window, then into the door frame. Leo managed to get the car started and put it in gear, but he was in a rush, hemmed in and crashed into a car that was parked in front of him. Simon was closing in. He tossed the empty pistol while unholstering a fresh gun and kept firing towards the car through the door frame. Leo rolled out of the driver's side, crouching by the back bumper and returned fire, bullets whizzing by Simon's head into the house behind him. He dove behind a car parked in the driveway and could see and hear footsteps slapping down the street.

Sirens began to wail from far away.

He ran limping to the front of the house and down the street watching for a sign in between the houses. A big dog started barking two doors down, a popping sound, the dog yelped once and was silent. He headed that way, gun out front and ready crouching behind cars as he went.

Glass breaking. A shrill shriek. Simon could see the motionless golden retriever at the front of the house, a curtain moved at the broken window. Sirens getting closer. He went to the side of the garage, he could hear a sound inside, a woman crying, sobbing, begging for her life.

Simon opened the side door, the garage was dimly lit. Leo was getting into the driver's side of the car while a woman was in the passenger's side.

"I'll kill her!" Leo shouted when he saw Simon in the doorway. The barrel of his gun was pressed against the side of her head while he tried to start the car with his left hand on the ignition key.

The car roared to life, and he revved the engine while keeping his eyes on Simon who did not move an inch.

"Open the damn garage door lady!" Leo shouted and she reached trembling hands up to the garage door opener that was clipped to the passenger side visor, pressed the button and the door began to roll up.

Simon did not move from the doorway, Leo kept his eyes on Simon, while his gun pressed against the woman's head did not move an inch either as the garage door completed it's opening, finally grinding to a halt.

Leo put the car in gear with his left hand, rolling out of the garage, eyes on Simon making sure he didn't make a move, then when the rear bumper was clear of the garage he put both hands on the wheel while punching down on the accelerator, but did not see Poet standing on the left side of the driveway with the pistol in his hand that fired two quick shots, POP, POP into the side of his face. The car shot across the street then veered to the right as Leo slumped to the side, slammed into a parked car, back tire burning rubber as Leo's foot with all his dead weight leaned down on it. Black smoke and screeching rubber filling the street with a horrible sound. The woman jumped out of the car running and stumbling away, too scared and out of breath to scream. Simon limped over with his pistol at the ready, pointed at the back of Leo's head, reached into the passenger side of the car and turned the ignition off.

Two cop cars came racing around the corner onto the street then braked to a stop. Poet and Simon laid their guns on the ground in front of them, took five steps back away and held their badges and ID's in their hands in the air. Two cops came out of each car, three of them with pistols in hand, one with a shotgun.

"We're police!" shouted Poet making sure

that his hands didn't move a single inch, and praying that they saw the badge in his outstretched hand.

"Alright, keep your hands up," shouted the lead cop as he trotted over to them with the barrel of his gun pointed up. He was talking into a mic on his collar as he slowed up and stood in front of Poet while another cop stood in front of Simon, both of them studying the badges and ID's. The cop with the shotgun went over to the smashed car and looked through the window at Leo slumped over the wheel, while the other cop went over to the crowd that had formed around the woman who got hijacked and was sitting on the ground in shock.

"Dispatch we have a Poetamos Jackson, San Francisco police department, and Simon Profit, FBI."

Poet looked over at Simon, narrowing his eyes, then walked over to him.

"What happened to Simon Profit, NYPD?"

Simon shrugged.

"Show me that badge," said Poet. He reached out and grabbed Simon's wrist with a vice grip and twisted it till he could see the front of the ID card.

There was a picture on Simon on the right, unsmiling wearing a black suit and tie, on the left a blue seal rimmed with gold with words going around it that said Department of Justice Federal Bureau of Investigation. In between the picture and the seal were big bold blue letters that read FBI. On the bottom was the sentence Special Agent and then a line with Simon's signature.

Poet sighed as though all the air that had ever existed in the entire atmosphere left his lungs. He'd been blindsided before, but never this flawlessly. It was the perfect crime. His partner for the past two days was a lying sonofabitch.

Half of him wanted to congratulate him on an excellent cover, and the other wanted to thrash him in the middle of the street.

"You're with the FBI?"

Simon nodded. "Behavioral analyst. I was a special agent for the past three years and they promoted me and gave me this for my first independent assignment. I couldn't tell you who I was because it might have compromised our little 'project'. I didn't want you to think I was somehow superior to you, because that might have affected your freethinking freewheeling attitude, which could have hindered your ability to flat out kick ass."

"You think a little title like behavioral analyst would make me think you were superior to me?" He started to chuckle, and could hardly catch his breath. "And hinder my ability to kick ass?"

"Behavioral analyst is at the top of the heap, I'll have you know. Only the most elite are invited to join this section of the FBI. We study criminals and anticipate crimes so we can prevent them before they happen."

"I'll invite you to do a behavioral analysis of the back of my hand in a minute."

"I knew you were going to say that."

"Man, you kidding me? FBI? You been lying to me this whole time, I should freewheel kick your butt all over this street."

"Hey guys," said the lead cop. "Sorry to butt in. Nice job getting that guy. Leo Andrade. He's been on the most wanted list for a few months, and from what that woman over there says, you saved her life."

"Yeah, well there's more to it," said Simon. "There's another dead body a few houses over. A woman who kidnapped a little girl. We have the girl and her mother at a motel nearby, we just need to have them transported to a safe location, and we'd like to assist to make sure it happens correctly."

Two more cop cars came onto the street, lights on, sirens blaring, even though all the real action was over. Cops loved sirens.

Simon limped down the street with the lead cop to the house where Leo's car was shot to pieces, then showed him where he went over the fence and the house where the old woman was.

He gave a complete statement with timelines and actions. His empty pistol lay on the ground and forensics came along and picked it up, putting it in a bag.

An ambulance came, two men in white coats put Leo in a black ziplock bag and took him away.

Then he and Poet rode in a squad car to the motel and retrieved Candace and Belina and went with them to the precinct. There was a distinct protocol in place for women and children who were victims of abuse. They said a quick goodbye, Candace gave each of them a big hug, and that was it.

Then they went back to the house on Calente avenue where Simon's car was parked, and the cops cut them loose.

"You gonna tell me the whole story now?" asked Poet.

"I'll tell you on the way to see Finke, how's that? You drive."

Simon opened the laptop while Poet drove through the streets towards the precinct. He typed quickly accessing financial databases.

"A few months ago we got a couple of red flags from this precinct. This is nothing new by the way. Whenever you get this much money involved, people are people. Temptations arise. A couple of drug busts that come up empty when all the intel is in place, crooks stealing from crooks happens all the time. But that stuff usually happens under the radar. We never know about it. In this precinct it was happening too many times. And then the Ranger got rolled. He was our guy, the drug investigators in that precinct thought he was their guy, but he was our plant. That's when I got involved. We weren't sure who it was, Boggs, Chubb or Finke, or maybe someone else down the food chain, or maybe a few of them. It still could be a few of them but it's too late now unless Finke wants to rat one of them out."

"He's the king rat?"

"As far as I'm concerned he is. And this is where it gets tricky. We need to cuff him before he can do something stupid."

"Like get away?"

"Yeah, that. He might have gotten wind that

Leo's dead and that we're the ones who got him. He might be making plans right about now."

"What kind of plans."

"The kind where he gets away forever. You know how many guys he put behind bars that'd love to see him eating lunch at the table next to them?"

"He wouldn't last a day."

"I have two federal marshals meeting us at the precinct in ten minutes. We either take him into custody or we don't get the chance. Finke holds the cards to this game now. It's up to him."

30.

They found a place to park in front and walked up the steps to the bullet proof doors and into the foyer. The clerk at the table was standing while the cop with the metal wand waited on the side. Two marshals dressed in green uniforms waited past the metal detecting gate. Both had pistols on their hips.

"Simon Profit, NYPD," said the clerk.

"FBI," said Simon showing the man his ID. "We need to go upstairs with those two officers."

"Yes, I know," said the clerk and waved them through.

The man with the metal detecting wand stood to the side to let them pass, emotionless.

They climbed the stairs to room 201, Simon first followed by the two marshals and then Poet.

The door was open. Finke sat behind the desk with a blank look on his face. He motioned for them to come inside and sit down. The two marshals came inside and flanked the doorway, hands resting on the handles of their pistols, straps off.

"Congratulations," said Finke. "You cracked the case."

"We're here to take you into custody," said Simon. "You're under arrest."

"For what?"

"Extortion, accessory to murder, accessory to kidnapping, taking bribes…"

"You don't have anything on me. You got Leo, he was the main criminal, him and Tang Tang running their crime enterprise from the comfort of his prison cell. I brought you in for a specific purpose and you achieved it, so congratulations again for a job well done."

"Yes. You're right about that," said Simon. "I'm sure we can work something out, get you a lighter prison sentence if you work with us. All you need to do is tell us who else in the precinct is involved. We can get to those little details later, but right now we need to take you into custody sir." Simon was polite. "This needs to be official so we can move forward lieutenant Finke."

"Again Mr. Profit, on what basis to you hinge your little fairy tale on?"

Simon opened the laptop pointing the screen towards Finke, holding it balanced on his left forearm while scrolling with his right forefinger showing bank accounts with balances and routing numbers.

"Nothing is secret in this world," said Simon. "You should know that. Here's two offshore accounts in the Cayman's. One for half a million, and the other with a million two hundred fifty thousand dollars. That's a lot of money for a lieutenant in a police department."

"It's not mine."

"We can prove that it is."

"Maybe I invested my money wisely. Maybe my ex-wife invested it for our retirement."

Simon scrolled. Images of Finke in a car with Candace putting her tongue near his ear.

"We accessed Leo's cloud account."

"A girl whispering in my ear isn't a crime."

Simon scrolled again. On the screen was a green digital line that spiked when the words were spoken.

"My deal with Tang was fifty grand per tip."

Simon could sense the change in Finke. His eyes slightly twitched, his left eyebrow lifted slightly, nostrils flared lightly on the edges, jaw slackened as his teeth unclenched.

"Don't do it," said Simon.

Finke was silent for a moment. His hands never came out from under the desk.

"We can have an agreement," said Simon. He began to speak in a calming tone of voice. Finke knew that he was finished as a cop, he just needed to be assured that he could go on living.

"All we need is your cooperation," continued Simon. "We have systems in place for situations like this."

"Would you go to hell for a single day if you knew you would be going to heaven the very next day anyways?" asked Finke. "Why would anyone in their right mind put up with a single moment of agony if they were going to die anyways? A man goes into the hospital with a fatal illness, knowing full well that he's never getting out alive. In a way that's how we all are in this life, wouldn't you all agree? Each and every one of us must pass the other side. We each have a fate that we cannot escape, and it's a fate that we all share."

Simon nodded. There was no getting away from this.

Finke pulled the short pistol out from under the desk. The marshals scrambled to pull their guns from their holsters, Poet tensed as he stood there ready to dive for cover, but Simon just stood there calmly as Finke put the gun scraping in between his teeth, pointed it at the roof of his mouth and pulled the trigger.

31.

Third floor of the FBI building in downtown Los Angeles, Simon sat down at a long table across from special agent Megan Acrillous, head of the witness protection program for the west coast.

She was tan and shiny as a fresh roasted walnut shell and looked about as hard. As though it would take a nut-cracker to get through her exterior. Good luck with anyone attempting that.

He showed her his badge and she studied it and his face for a moment before tapping the stack of papers in front of her.

"This file's closed," she said definitively. "Candace will testify in a court of law that she witnessed her husband Tang Tang Fernandez and Leo Andrade murder two men at the strip club two years ago, and in exchange for that testimony we'll put her and her daughter in the witness protection program for the rest of her life, or as long as she chooses. We found the blood DNA at the club on the floor, and in the car that was used to transport the body, but without an actual body, it was all just circumstantial evidence. But with an eyewitness testimony, we're going to lock up Tang Tang for a very long time."

"I'd like to see her one more time before she heads out," said Simon.

"You think that's a good idea?" asked Megan. She studied him carefully. She was a trained criminal psychoanalyst, could read the slightest body language and facial expressions and tell what emotions a person was internalizing.

Simon though at the moment was a blank slate. As though he wasn't even alive. Like a rock you picked up from the desert floor. She couldn't even tell if he was breathing. And yet, there might be the slightest raising of his eyebrow on the right side.

"You know," she said. "After everything she's been through, and the change that's coming up, we usually don't like to put any potential emotional stumbling blocks if you will, in front of people."

"Yeah, I understand," said Simon. "Your call. You're in charge." He was silent for moment, thinking about it. "I did save her you know."

Grasping at straws.

It was her job to keep the task at hand, to keep the process moving forward, but he had a point. He did save her and had some rights in the process.

"What do you want to get out of this?" she asked.

He took a deep breath and sighed. There it

was, thought Megan, a clear signal. Fear of loss, loneliness, heartache, maybe a twinge of devotion, the other half of what most people called love. It wasn't the thought of a situation that was in his mind when he sighed, it was the thought of her.

He nodded as he made up his mind of what he wanted to say.

"In this business we're in. There's no real satisfaction, and how can there be? You stop one criminal, another one pops up to take its place. I say 'it' because in my mind they become like objects, non-human, soulless, like robots, or puppets doing the bidding of some type of master. You solve one crime and another one or two or three materialize as though out of nowhere, because where can they come from except some sort of ethereal world that's not even connected to the one we live in, as though it was oozing from some crack in the mantle of the earth, oozing from a filthy sewer pit, contaminating paradise. With everything we're given in this world, the miracle of it all..."

He shook his head and took another deep breath with a sigh, looked away from her and gazed out the window.

"Aren't you getting a little emotional?" she asked. "You're a trained professional. A cop. You're supposed to be immunized, inoculated from feelings of remorse from the criminal element that's surrounding you, that you're battling, immunized from the disease that you're fighting against, desensitized from its malevolent effects."

He continued to look out the window while he spoke.

"Not one bit of this world was made or conceived by any one of us. And yet every once in a while, some people call it Déjà vu, some people might never experience it, they might walk through their entire lives without thinking for even the briefest of moments that there was something under the surface of everything, something unseen, pure... "

"You're in love with her."

He turned to look her straight in the eyes.

"So what if I am." A statement.

"That makes things a little more difficult. You know."

"Why." It was a statement again, not a question. As though he was answering himself with a proclamation. A declaration. "Why would my feelings for her make any situation in the world more difficult."

She had to be blunt.

"Because she might not feel the same way."

It was true. He nodded in agreement.

"Shouldn't we at least give her that chance?"

His face became firm, she could see the determination set in his jaw and the corners of his eyes, and then it all slackened in an instant, a release from internal pressure.

It was a tell-tale sign, the acceptance of fate. She had to be blunt again.

"For her own sake, for her safety, *if* you really do have true feelings for her, you need to forget about yourself and only think about what's best for her. And right now, the safest thing for her is to disappear."

"Can you think of anyone else in the world she'd be safer with than me?"

"Living in the open with you by her side? You'd both be sitting ducks. You're not superman, no one is. It'd only be a matter of time."

"I'm not talking about living in the open."

"You'd have to give up everything forever."

"The way I look at it, I'd be gaining everything forever."

She shook her head and continued.

"No more being a cop. No power. No more being the guy with the badge who can bust you and put you in prison. No more control. I'm just being up front here with you Simon. You'd have to learn how to be a small-fry, a little guy, a nobody."

"You don't know me very well, I never thought of myself as a tough guy that someone had to be afraid of, I never used the badge to hide behind and abuse people."

"You might not realize it, but you have a certain, how do we say look about you."

"What do you mean by that?"

"You *look* like a cop. You've got it in your eyes. How you manage to operate undercover is beyond me."

"Some people say I look like a criminal. Depends on who you ask."

"In my opinion you'd stand out like a sore thumb."

"Don't you think a single mother with a young child moving into a town all alone would attract attention?"

"A single mother with a young child is more normal than you'd think these days, unfortunately."

"I can blend in, get a job as a mechanic or a carpenter, or a plumber or an electrician."

She sighed.

"Well, we can't control her personal life and tell her who she can and can't be with. And we also can't protect her forever if she doesn't take our advice."

She studied his face. He could tell from experience that she was psychoanalyzing his muscle tension, jaw placement, eye movements.

"You ever heard of the Stockholm syndrome?"

"Of course."

"Where a captive and a captor form an emotional bond?"

"Where are you going with this?"

"It works for the person who saves the person from captivity also. In some cases the person saving the other person from harm can form an intense attraction. They have protected the person from destruction and they have an internal *need* to continue the protection. They can't help it. You, Simon, are exhibiting classic behavioral signs of this syndrome. It's like you're under some type of hypnosis."

"You know my name. You know who I am. You know my credentials."

"Special agent Simon Profit. You've worked for the FBI for the past three years and you're a behavioral analyst. Congratulations that's quite an achievement. Still, it doesn't make you immune to this type of behavior. You're still human. She's really quite a beautiful woman. It's easy to see how you or any man for that matter could become attracted to her."

"I can't deny that she's nice to look at," said Simon. "Or the fact that we spent some time together in an intense life or death situation. Of course those two factors would make me feel me more attracted to her than in a normal circumstance. Putting a label on the outcome doesn't make it any less real. There is a human emotion when someone is pleasing to the eyes, and it's not always lust, sometimes it can't be defined. This is something more than that. I can't describe it."

"I'll tell you what," said Megan. "Sometimes my better judgement is no better than anyone else in this world. You're a trained professional who can do a self-analysis. It's her choice. We can only provide protection to someone who wants it. If you're part of the equation so be it."

"Thank you."

She picked up the phone and spoke quietly to someone on the other end, giving instructions, then hung up and looked at Simon with solemn eyes.

"She's on her way, you can use this room and take as much time as you need."

32.

"So you know the deal? You're okay with everything?"

Simon studied her face across the table. Still to this day he'd never seen a more angelic face. Soft raised cheekbones, big round dark eyes framed by silky black hair.

She shrugged, and her face suddenly looked tired. "I read the papers. They explained it all to me."

She studied his eyes. Waiting for him to continue.

"It's pretty simple," said Simon. "They give you and Belina a new identity, put you in some town in the middle of nowhere, in the middle of the country, give you a steady stream of money to live on, you get a job, Belina goes to school, and you live a normal life."

"Yes, a normal life," she said. Her gaze went to the window, out into the clouds with a wistful look. "What about Tang Tang, the club, the other girls?"

"Tang Tang's been charged with bribery,

extortion, money laundering, kidnapping, and accessory to murder for the two guys in the club you witnessed. We think he'll get fifteen to twenty years. It's the best they could do. The other girls have scattered to the wind. The club is being sold."

"Who's buying it?"

"A non-profit."

"Are they going to tear it down?"

He shook his head.

"No, they're not going to tear it down, they're going to renovate it."

"They should bulldoze it," she said. "Find the biggest bulldozer in the whole world, grind up every inch of that building, smash it all down and take it to the dump, then dig up all the concrete and asphalt surrounding it, every speck of dust that touched that place, and bring in fresh new dirt from the mountains, make a park with trees and grass. That's what they should do."

"That's an expensive building," said Simon.

"Yes," she said. "It was." She closed her eyes trying to erase the scars.

"The non-profit is going to make a freedom center."

"What's that?"

"You'll like this plan. In some ways they will be bulldozing the building. They'll go in and tear down all the interior walls, swamp it out with a fire hose, disinfect the entire place with pure bleach, but keep the exterior walls and roof, and rebuild it from the inside out."

"You didn't answer my question. What's a

freedom center?"

He was straightforward.

"It's for women who've been abused, exploited for money, dehumanized, reduced to a commodity for sale. Women who have been enslaved."

"Like me," she said.

"Yeah. Like you. Anyways, these people are coming in with a lot of good money and they're going to ransack that place, tear out all the bad and replace it with all the good."

"So that's Tang Tang and the club," she said. "Leo's gone, but Tang Tang will send someone else after me."

"His assets are frozen. The feds are going after everything he has. They'll confiscate everything for non-payment of taxes. He won't have a penny left, and bad guys don't work for free."

Her eyes gazed out the window.

"Candace, look at me for a moment."

"Yes," her eyes drifted back towards him. They were suddenly tired, withdrawn, lifeless.

"I have a proposal."

She studied him, waiting for it in silence.

"I'll go with you. Into hiding. Into the witness protection program. I can be your protector."

She didn't say anything for a moment, and yet her eyes softened.

"I can be your extra layer of safety. I'll protect you."

It wasn't enough.

"We can be a real family, you and me and Belina."

Her eyes shifted, blinked, he could see a veiled hidden fear, and not for her or Belina, but for him. His proposal hung in the air like a dark cloud on a dreary day.

"I can't do it," she said finally. "Not yet. I'm thankful that you saved me, and Belina. You must know that I'm forever in your debt."

He shook his head. That was the one statement he didn't want to hear.

"You don't owe me a single thing Candace. Ever. We just happened to come together for some strange reason, and I don't want it to end. So maybe in a way I'm just being selfish, just thinking about myself. Megan Acrillous warned me and I didn't listen."

Her face softened as she understood what he was telling her without him putting it into words.

"I do care about you," she said. "As much as I can I suppose. I've been a hostage for the past four years. A prisoner in a grimy dungeon. I went from an innocent high school girl with flowers in my hair to a dirty stripper in the blink of an eye."

He shook his head. "No..."

She smiled gently at him.

"I know what I was. And it's going to take a little bit of time to wash away those memories. I can't be with anybody except Belina for a while, I know that. I want to live through her, and with her, and be a little girl again, in a way, read stories and play in the yard, I hope we have a white picket fence. Play with dolls, paint with water colors all day, maybe get a puppy, or a kitten. Fill our days with wonder and magic, rainbows and flowers."

He smiled. It sounded wonderful. There was no room for a big stinky clunky guy in that fairy tale adventure. It was time for him to step away.

Simon walked back to the car and got into the driver's seat. Poet was studying him. Waiting for him to say something but he just sat there staring straight out the windshield with his hand on the ignition key, his brain in neutral, gears disengaged. It was an easily translatable facial expression. Hang-dog bubble burst disbelief defeat when a girl says no.

"So what's the story?"

"She'll call me in a year."

Poet looked at him in disbelief while slowly shaking his head. There was no way he was going to sugar coat it, that strategy never worked. Tell it like it is, or don't tell it at all. If someone is your friend, truly your friend, you hit them over the head with the truth and don't mamby-pamby it. Poet sighed deeply with disappointment both for his friend, and for himself, before he got out the obligatory sledge hammer.

"Man, why'd you have to fall in love in with a stripper?"

"I didn't plan on it." He sighed, then said, "I'm an idiot."

"They say that's the first step on the road to enlightenment. The fool thinks he's a wise man, but the wiseman knows himself to be a fool."

"I wish you wouldn't quote Shakespeare to me right now. But if what he said is true, I must be the wisest man in the world. Because right now I feel like the stupidest person to ever walk the earth."

"Well I have to admit she is damn pretty nice. And she's not even a stripper anymore right? Probably never really was. Forced into it by circumstances. She was just going through a phase in her life and now she's out of it. Forever. My question though to you should be how in the world can you fall for a woman that you've only been near enough to talk to for about five hours?"

"I don't know, I'm an idiot remember?"

"Granted that five total hours was spread out over two days from the first time we saw her at the club till just now, but man, you don't wait around."

"A lot can happen quickly I guess. And to be honest with you, I don't even really know what happened. All I know is I feel like I got hit by a truck. I guess I'll be alright."

"Damn right you will be."

"Okay tough guy. How long did you know your wife before you got married?"

"Five years."

"Took you *that* long to figure it out?"

"Didn't seem that long."

"Half a decade isn't a long time?"

"Well I guess if you put it that way."

"Five years is one twentieth of a century."

"Okay I get the point."

"Five years, five hours. I don't think the amount of time is the determining factor. And in my case, I do and she don't."

"Sometimes it's best to take your time. Man, Simon, you gotta give her some real time. You know what I mean? Some real alone time. Look at what she just got out of. You kidding me? If she needs a year, give her a year. Get yourself a hobby to take your mind off it."

"A hobby?"

"Yeah, a simple past-time, a diversion, the time will fly by. That's my advice to you."

"Yeah well, I guess it's advice I'll have to take whether I like it or not. I don't really matter in the equation anymore, and that's okay with me. The most important thing is she'll be alright."

"Someone once said that in love and revenge, a woman is more barbaric than any man."

"I've heard it. That's probably why a lot of men would rather be in a war than be in love. That's kind of weird, me saying that for some reason."

"You're not turning weak are you? Maybe the best thing is for you to go bust someone. Let's take a ride and find some criminals and drag 'em into the jail house. That'll make you feel better. They're everywhere out there if you know where to find them. C'mon man, let's go hunting. If we're lucky we'll find someone that wants to resist arrest."

Simon shook his head.

"You know, we have some unfinished business."

"Those guys at the dock?"

"Yeah, those guys."

Poet clapped his hands together.

"Now you're talking! Heck yeah, let's go round 'em up."

"Too late, it's already happening."

"What the hell you talking about?"

Poet narrowed his eyes as Simon started the car and pulled into traffic.

"Just sit back and enjoy the ride and we'll take a ride out to the coast."

33.

Twenty minutes later, Simon pulled up a few doors down from a house in Long Beach. Poet recognized it as the first house they went to with Fred when he was still alive. The first house occupied by one of the dumbass dock workers who were going to help some gangsters rob a container from a ship for a little bit of side money.

Two police cars and three big black SUV's with tinted windows were sitting in front of the geniuses' house.

A couple of guys with black jackets and big bold yellow letters spelling out FBI were escorting a man from the front door with his hands behind his back while neighbors on all sides around the house mulled around watching.

Another man with a badge hanging down from around his neck holding an automatic rifle stood in the middle of the street and held his hand out in the universal sign to stop.

Simon put the car in park, turned the engine

off, got out and showed him his badge and his ID. The other man recognized him and managed a slight smile. Poet got out of the car and walked towards the front bumper.

"This is my partner Detective Jackson."

The man with the rifle just nodded and went back to minding the street. Armed backup in case someone tried something stupid, tried to intervene in the arrest that was taking place on an otherwise quiet residential street.

"FBI," said Poet shaking his head.

"Yes," said Simon. "And I'm inviting you to join us. I head up a special department. They send me places, and into situations that need a little extra finesse. We did pretty well on this case, you and me, and it didn't take very long to crack it."

Poet looked away. It was a great opportunity and he knew it.

They watched Nick Fangano get loaded into one of the big SUV's, silver handcuffs behind his back while his wife of ten years, and three kids ages eight to ten huddled off to the side crying while watching their daddy get hauled away.

"Poor bastard," said Poet.

"It's a good lesson for those kids," said Simon. "Crime doesn't pay."

"So now what?"

"Now you go home to your wife and spend some time in peace and comfort. When you're ready, if you want, you can join me at the bureau. Pure and simple."

"I meant, now what for you."

"For me?" asked Simon. It wasn't a question

for him as much as it was the beginning of a statement of fact. "Plato once said that only the dead have seen the end of the war."

Poet thought for a moment and then nodded before replying.

"Our job never ends."

The implication was not lost on Simon.

Our job he said. Maybe someday they'd be a team again.

They drove in silence back to Poet's car parked where they'd left it the day before.

"Don't you want to take a plane or something?"

"And leave this fine auto behind?" said Poet. "It's only four hundred miles to San Francisco. I'll be there a little after midnight. You know I'll probably go see my dad when I get back home. I'll tell him I worked with someone who might know as much about Shakespeare as he does."

Simon shook his head.

"I don't pretend to be a professor. I just know a few lines that were written by a guy who's been dead four hundred years. They kind of stuck in me like a plate of spaghetti get sticks in your gut when you eat too much of it. Knowing a line and knowing what's in between them, knowing the meaning behind the words is night and day. It's like a cheap trick, pulling up a phrase like a human recorder. Like a robot."

"I don't believe it," said Poet. "And I don't think you do either. This whole thing played out like some sort of real life tragedy. And it was strange being in the middle of it, now that I look back. Seems like I've been on edge every minute for the past two days."

"Welcome to the FBI."

"Not just yet," said Poet. "I'll think about it."

"Don't overthink it.

"You think about this one pal. 'Heat not a furnace so hot for your foe that you singe yourself'."

"Henry VIII. Act one, scene one. And then, Norfolk says to Buckingham, by violent swiftness, that which we run at, and lose by overrunning. It's a good line. Henry the eighth was a bad-ass king, but he's been dead for a long time, and now just comes to life as a character in a play. In essence be careful stirring up trouble and don't get too far ahead of yourself. Don't worry Poet, I'll try to stay out of trouble."

Poet reached over, shook Simon's hand without another word, then got out of the car and walked towards the little sedan without looking back.

Simon shouted out the open window.

"I'll get the agency to buy you a new car!"

Poet stuck the back of his right hand in the air with his index, middle, and ring fingers extended and kept walking.

Simon could almost hear Poet telling him to read between the lines, then as soon as he saw that Poet was able get the car started he drove away and headed towards the monoliths.

Skyscrapers in the middle of the city looming in the distance, golden sunset reflecting off mirrored windows fifty stories and more high.

He drove until it was almost dark, looking for a forgotten corner of the world, then parked on a deserted side street next to a fence topped with barbed wire, windblown trash stuck in the bottom of the fence, broken bottles littering the dirty sidewalk that at one point in time must have been newly poured concrete, sparkling clean, the envy of the neighborhood and a job well done by a proud group of construction workers with hard hats and boots.

On one corner up ahead sat a liquor store lonely and forlorn, with one solitary loiterer leaning against the corner, smoking something, looking at nothing, waiting for anything. It was a slow night. Every now and then he'd shuffle his feet and take a toke of the blunt in between his finger and thumb, then switch shoulders leaning against the bricks on the corner of the store.

Simon marveled at the sight. He looked at his watch. It was nearly seven o'clock. The dark of night descending on the city. Ten hours till dawn. Eight thousand seven hundred sixty hours left in the year.

That was a long time to wait around.

Maybe Candace would reconsider the whole year thing, and call him to her home tonight or tomorrow, but then again, maybe she was gone forever. Time would tell, and yet how to fill that immense vacuum of time without dwelling on it? He could be like the guy leaning against the corner of the store shifting shoulders when one got tired, minute after empty minute and let his thoughts drift into nothingness, sublime content, conscious of his breathing, and gravity holding him to the earth and nothing more.

Nothing less.

Plato once said that the greatest wealth was to live content with little. And Socrates advised to 'beware the barrenness of a busy life'.

They were advocating a solemn unburdened life in order to internalize self-knowledge and worth, rather than projecting it and dissipating it to the void surrounding you, as though your thoughts were the atmosphere of the planet leaking into space.

And yet it was Nietzsche who asked:

"Is life not a thousand times too short for us to bore ourselves?"

Simon pulled the Glock from the glove compartment, checked the clip, put it in the shoulder holster under his jacket, then put an extra clip of bullets in one pocket, the hand held taser in another, and the billy club in his back pocket, got out of the car, took one last look at the guy standing with his shoulder against the corner of the wall, and began to walk in the other direction into the deepening night.